The Guy that Does the Thing

OBSERVATIONS,
DELIBERATIONS,
AND CONFESSIONS,
VOLUME 11

Divine Creases

a novel of sorts

W. C. ANDREW GROOME

iUniverse®

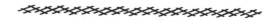

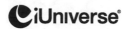

THE GUY THAT DOES THE THING - OBSERVATIONS, DELIBERATIONS, AND CONFESSIONS VOLUME 11

iUniverse books may be ordered through booksellers or by contacting:

iUniverse
1663 Liberty Drive
Bloomington, IN 47403
www.iuniverse.com
1-800-Authors (1-800-288-4677)

ISBN: 978-1-4917-5810-6 (sc)
ISBN: 978-1-4917-5808-3 (e)

Library of Congress Control Number: 2013923793

Print information available on the last page.

iUniverse rev. date: 2/24/2015

I am extremely grateful to everyone who has been a part of my journey. There are too many to mention and I cannot imagine that mentioning them would help them in any way. The sentiment that I am comfortable with is that I am showing my loved ones the greatest respect by not mentioning them - at least not while you are still alive.

In Dedication to, and in Loving Memory of one of the last suffragettes. A tried and true Ohio Democrat with a sincere passion for the efforts of Franklin Delano Roosevelt. It was her outlook on life that produced two solid conservative Ohio Republicans which set off a chain of events that led to me meeting my wife. I am eternally grateful to have known you. Thank you for the socks at Christmas and the chicken wings you made during your visits. I even miss you calling me "Fatty."

Dorothy Louise Rothe

January 4, 1915 – August 30, 2014

Disclaimer

The text that follows is art in the sense that one, or more ideas became something that could be produced and packaged as a product.

The author brings forth these ideas because the author feels compelled to do so. The inspiration for these ideas has been the subject of many therapy sessions and attending psychologists have made several statements that these stories and characters are all in the author's head.

Regardless of the source, the author believes the intent of these ideas is to help the author understand something that is really worth understanding, though at present, has no idea of what that might be.

The compulsion to articulate the ideas for entertainment purposes is derived from an understanding that this is what the author is supposed to do right now.

There is no opinion expressed herein and there is nothing that the author would ever assert as fact.

This is a book. If reading the book seems to help you in some way, then the author is glad. If reading this book does not help you, the author can understand why such is the case but makes no apologies. Either way, there is nothing in this book worth getting upset or suing over.

See Volume 17

As a student in the public school and university systems, everything I wrote was in the quest for the "perfect paper" as judged by the people who had the job of judging me. Whether the task was a term paper, written exam, or a report, I endeavored to ease the minds of the judges by presenting an organized review of the material in which the judges were interested in a manner that was exactly as they wanted to see it. That approach to writing carried over into my career as a consulting engineer.

My first book, "Ripple," was written with the audience in mind. Some of the people that would be reading the book were written about in the book, and I knew I would see them again someday. Then I retired. In the first year of retirement, I wrote my second book. During the process, I became aware of the entangled mess of how difficult it is to say something you believe is important within a construct that is fictional, satirical, or one of the other 'als. I know real authors do it all the time, which starts to explain why many of the authors of great fiction that we have come to admire were nut jobs. During the process of telling the story I wanted to tell, giving the characters names and writing dialogue were constant hurdles and unnecessary impediments to progress. One of the approaches to find a way around those hurdles was to uniquely identify each Fictional Character with a number and represent them in the book in a shorthand notation, i.e., FicChaTen. If you are paying attention, you will see a pattern to my FicCha designations.

Certain characters were given more human names because these are the characters I want the audience to make a real connection with over time. But they too are represented in a shorthand notation. For example, TGTDTT is "The Guy That Does The Thing;" OBandSD is "Old Beach and Surfer Dude."

The way I addressed the dialogue issue was to present the conversations in a script format. From time to time, I add some description amidst the dialogue, but for the most part, it is just these people talking and this is what I have decided that they said. I have deliberately left several places throughout the first book, and now this one, for the reader, you, to fill in the rest of the picture. For example, one reader would imagine a conversation in which one or more of the people were screaming. Another reader, reading the same dialogue, might imagine that the people were just talking to each other. But there are also readers who would begin to pick up on the rhythmic nature of the dialogue and the ranges of vocals, and the scene becomes something that would rival the work of Andrew Lloyd Webber. Throughout the book, you could take on the various personas of the readers I just described. I figured that since my mind set and frame of reference were all over the place during the course of writing this book, there is a good chance that your mind set and frame of reference will shift and drift as you read it.

As I became comfortable with the way I was dealing with fictional characters and the conversations they might have, I felt a growing sense of freedom with respect to every single other facet of writing a fictional book. I decided that I was going to write what I wanted to write how I wanted to write it. As long as it makes sense to me, it stays. The critics, in all their various forms, will be given no voice in what I was about to create. The only exceptions were a small circle of people who will not criticize, but make the changes to make the final product better.

The resulting approach to dealing with fictional characters, dialogue, and certain terms was implemented in the first book of "The Guy That Does The Thing" series which is "The Guy That Does The Thing – Observations, Deliberations, and Confessions Volume 17" by me and is "improved upon" in this volume. Since that is where it all started, that is where you go to find out why it is this way now. But, to get you started in the book you are holding:

TGTDTT	The Guy That Does The Thing. Introduced in Volume 17.
OBandSD	Old Beach and Surfer Dude. Introduced in Volume 17.
FicCha	Fictional Character. The concept was introduced in Volume 17 and carried over into this publication. For the most part, FicChaTen in the last book is the same FicChaTen in this book. What I can tell you is that FicChaZero always refers to the same character, regardless of the volume in which it appears.

I did retire the brackets, [], as they were superfluous and actually hindered the reader. It made sense in my thinking when I created Volume 17, but like training wheels, I no longer need them in my writing. There is universal agreement among my inner circle that I was late in retiring the brackets. But in my defense, an editable version was provided to two people for final edits and they left the brackets in. It is done. I am a wiser man for having done it.

There is more but you get the point.

To get Volume 17 and any of my other books, check out the web site www.TheGuyThatDoesTheThing.com.

W.C. Andrew Groome

August2014

An Anecdote to prepare your palate

The Narrator

As one story goes, in the beginning, God created the heavens and the earth. God created a whole bunch of stuff that was going to be born, live, and then die with the cycles of nature and time on Earth. Then, in a moment of inspiration (Where does God look for inspiration or where does the inspiration come from?), God creates a creature that is intended to be master of the earth and all the stuff that God created. God then decides that this creature needs a complementary creature so that it doesn't look for complements from any of the stuff that was just created.

The Creature and its Complement begin what is assumed to be an eternal existence, with a sense of peace and total satisfaction. The Creature thought life was good and the Complement had no counter argument to put forth.

Then one day Complement goes for a walk and hears a voice. According to the story, the voice is coming from a snake in a tree. The voice says to Complement that God was fearful that Complement might eat from the "Tree of Knowledge" because it would make Complement as powerful as God, and God doesn't want that.

Complement	All that I imagine that I could ever need or desire is to come from God as long as Creature and I do not eat the fruit from the "Tree of Knowledge." I am happy and content.
Voice	Oh, but you really aren't. You will never know the joy of child birth or the pleasure of sex, for that matter. Imagine feeling better than you do right now. All you have to do is pluck and bite. Then you will no longer be beholden to God's Grace in the pursuit of your desires.
(Brief Pause)	
Complement	Now that you mention it, maybe I am not as happy as I should be and who does God think he is anyway? But still, you are asking me to take a big risk. I have it pretty good right now.
Voice	Don't you understand? Now that you know what I have told you, you will never be content. Your choice no longer exists.
The Narrator	Complement began to ponder. The pondering became feeling. The feeling became overwhelming. And for the first time, Complement felt passion. Sensations began to come to her mind from parts of her body that she did not understand why she had anyway. It was time to find out why the Complement was built the way she was built and no god is going to hide that information from her.
Complement	Give me the apple.

Election Night Part 2

Weather Report Fujiwhara Beach, FL

	Actual	Avg.	Record
Mean Temperature	74 °F		
Max Temperature	79 °F	77 °F	86 °F (2002)
Min Temperature	69 °F	66 °F	55 °F (1999)
Dew Point	61 °F		
Average Humidity	63		
Maximum Humidity	88		
Minimum Humidity	51		
Precipitation	0.03 in		
Sea Level Pressure	30.14 in		
Wind Speed	17 mph (NE)		
Max Wind Speed	28 mph		
Max Gust Speed	40 mph		
Visibility	10 miles		
Events	Rain		

TGTDTT I hate making decisions.

This was the first Election Night of all the Election Nights in the adult life of TGTDTT that he was not holding an alcoholic beverage in his hand. In the past, Election Night was as good excuse as any to experience the faux euphoria attributed to the perceived effects of biologically processing the products of one or more distilleries. TGTDTT hasn't quit drinking, he just has a much shorter list of reasons to drink than he used to have. Today, the only reason TGTDTT drinks is because he chooses to and he chooses not to drink as he watches a partial reboot of government. TGTDTT wanted his mind sharp. When the dust settles on this election, decisions have to be made.

TGTDTT hates making decisions because it relies on a pure

motivation that TGTDTT is unwilling to believe he has. It is so much easier to do what others ask you to do than it is to make a choice. TGTDTT never argued the merits or virtue of using alcohol to enhance an experience, but decisions require a clear mind and a pure soul to be really good decisions, and alcohol is an impediment to having a clear mind or a pure soul.

The votes have been cast and counted. The results are in and various elected government positions are being filled or re-filled. At the federal level, there was no upsetting the apple cart. The expectation is that the federal government is going to seize larger percentages of the Gross National Product in order to respond to a greater dependency of its citizens and the need to control their behavior in order to stay within budget. At the state level, some of the "good guys" replaced some of the "old guys" but the general thinking of how best to deal with the continued encroachments to "state's rights" by the federal government is not expected to improve. At the county and city levels, there is no hope for a better world. Elections are still a vanity exercise for the people who have "made it," and for the most part, the electorate remains unwilling to educate themselves on issues, allowing the same old chaff to "serve" them as elected officials ... Einstein was SOOO right about the definition of insanity!

TGTDTT watched the fifty-two inch flat-screen television tuned to the regional news channel. Between the segments involving the news anchors trying to fill air time, the producer cuts to various roving reporters giving a first-hand account of activities at polling places, various government offices, and, most importantly, the hotel ballrooms where the candidates are either celebrating their victory or thanking supporters for a well fought campaign.

It occurred to TGTDTT that it seems inappropriate to view a political campaign as a fight unless none of the candidates are really speaking the absolute truth. "He said, she said" goes out the window when at least one person in the conversation has mastery of the subject matter. A political campaign is a competition in the sense that the candidate with the most votes wins. But if at least one candidate was clear in mind and pure in soul, all of the other candidates would get out of the race. The only time in the history of this country that TGTDTT knows of such a thing happening is the election of the first President of the United States of America. Once George Washington paved the way, other people thought they could do a better job, and there were also people who thought someone else would do a better job. Today people of all walks of life believe they can do a better job than people who currently hold office. But yet, there is no coherent argument that these people who get elected are better at anything other than getting the voter to believe things that just aren't true.

Today, it is understood that public service is a way to plug into the system to manifest your particular world view. Your world view could be to get yours, to get even, or to get more. Regardless of why, people run for office to get theirs, to get even, or to get more. The voters decide who gets to plug in at certain spots and the voters cast their votes for the same reasons as the candidates run for office. The voters have to believe the candidate deserves to be elected because it will serve their world view. Increasingly, the voters' world view is a perception that their lives are overwhelming and they are reaching out for any help they can get from anybody who is offering ... or they are simply carrying out what they perceive to be their "civic duty" to vote, regardless of their knowledge of either the issues or the candidates (sometimes it's just easier to listen to friends who listen to friends who listen to friends ... you get the drift). For the "ruling class," that phenomenon is priceless.

In the abstract, the "Tree of Knowledge" has been replaced with something more parental. But the story is essentially the same and the results are predictable. Anytime a voice says "All will be better if you do what I say" to a person who is unable or unwilling to recognize it for the lie that it is, that person ends up worse off and filled with remorse while the voice has moved on to other people.

TGTDTT accepts that is the way it is today and that it is better than the way it used to be. Elections are child's play compared to revolutions, coups, and assassinations. Things have gotten better, but people are still incredibly "stoopid" in the sense that they are willing to devote their lives to a set of rules that have exceptions and contradictions. These people seem to think that a person can write down a set of words that nullify natural phenomena and when things get worse, because worse is what happens when you attempt to defy nature, these people think we all need to try harder.

At the heart of the matter is the collection of words that someone wrote down that force you and I to do things we would not otherwise do and cannot understand why we are forced to do those things in the first place. The extent of our collective confusion and frustration is manifested as noise in the communication channel, and that noise has the ability to impact costs and revenues of the people who write the words we are told to live by.

When the amount of noise gets to a certain level, someone writes down some more words that sets off a course of events intended to convince you and I that these words that are written down are really good words. You and I just need to try harder. There are entire libraries of words that people believe contains more truth than a single high school physics book. But unless one of the books in one of the libraries is a high school physics book, it probably doesn't.

People in government, at all levels and organizations, write words that seize assets and redistribute those assets in accordance with another set of words. When the assets seized by government are less than the government's intentions, government writes words that "authorize" the seizure of additional assets. When the people who write words for government are replaced through elections, term limits, indictments, retirement or transition to beyond the physical realm, more words are written to redefine government's intentions with respect to the distribution of seized assets.

The voters cast their votes for candidates in the hope that the words that end up being written will fill a need that they might have using the assets government has seized. Some voters hope their votes will produce words that fewer assets are seized, or at least the assets they own will not be seized. Some voters hope their votes will produce words that allow government to seize more assets from "other people" to buy something they want to have bought for themselves ... but they want to use other people's cash to buy or provide what they want (a great gig if you're part of the ruling class ... or maybe even if you suck up the same).

Increasingly (and today a majority of) voters want words that will alleviate their worries and concerns. The voters are babies who just want to be held and provided for. Voters want to feel safe and cared for because they crave the feeling of being loved. The votes cast for a candidate are the offerings from the people to their gods. The office the candidate is running for is their place in the pecking order of gods.

In Fujiwhara Beach, there are five people who have been empowered through the majority support of the voters to look out for our best interests and keep us safe. In Mosquito County, there are five people who have a similar set of responsibilities for the unincorporated areas. There are five more who are entrusted with the education of our children. From there we have people who vote for words at the state level and then the federal level. But don't forget about other political word writing offices like the Attorney General, Sherriff, County Clerk, or Property Appraiser. Each of these people will then hire other people to do their bidding who will hire others who will hire others ... all of them unelected overseers of the masses who write the words. The journey from your home town to the oval office via the corridors of government can take many paths and every government office is access controlled. All of these people have control over our lives and the voters gave it to them.

It is TGTDTT's theory that somewhere in the recesses of the brain, there is a crease that holds, or is intended to hold, the information that allows a person to feel safe by putting all their trust in God and consider it wrong to have government try to love us. Wrong like the kinds of things that happen when a sheep herder has been out on the range with the flock a little longer than one might think necessary. The problem is that most of the people who vote these days don't have that crease. That crease either did not form at all or something has damaged it or it has become superfluous like the appendix.

But in some respects, things have gotten better or more advanced which means that people have the capacity to learn. Learning puts creases in the brain. Is it possible that people could learn the bits and pieces needed to crease their brains in just the right spot, and just the right way, so that we, as a society, stop electing douche bags who make life worse for just about everyone (under the auspices of "caring" for its citizens)?

FicChaZero	Things must be this way until they are different.
TGTDTT	It is all the filters, the fears, the lack of trust they have in someone such as yourself.
FicChaZero	Why do you trust me?
TGTDTT	I trust who I hope you are.
FicChaZero	That seems fair.

Election Day minus 90 days

Weather Report Northfield, VT

Actual	Avg.	Record	
Mean Temperature	59 °F	66 °F	
Max Temperature	74 °F	78 °F	91 °F (2001)
Min Temperature	44 °F	55 °F	40 °F (1951)
Dew Point	47 °F		
Average Humidity	69		
Maximum Humidity	100		
Minimum Humidity	38		
Precipitation	0.00 in	0.15 in	2.28 in (1990)
Sea Level Pressure	30.15 in		
Wind Speed	2 mph (South)		
Max Wind Speed	10 mph		
Max Gust Speed	24 mph		
Visibility	6 miles		
Events	Fog		

Weather Report Fujiwhara Beach, FL

Actual	Avg.	Record	
Mean Temperature	84 °F		
Max Temperature	86 °F	85 °F	93 °F (2010)
Min Temperature	81 °F	75 °F	73 °F (1997)
Dew Point	74 °F		
Average Humidity	74		
Maximum Humidity	82		
Minimum Humidity	62		
Precipitation	0.00 in		
Sea Level Pressure	30.03 in		
Wind Speed	9 mph (ESE)		
Max Wind Speed	18 mph		
Max Gust Speed	-		
Visibility	10 miles		
Events	None		

The Dr. Charles Lectures - A Long Time Ago

In the spirit of paying honor to the writers and actors in the cinematic genius of "Back to School" starring the late Rodney Dangerfield, we have a small isolated college where the "nobody kids" of the Nuevo-riche in nowhere towns spend four to five years and a chunk of daddy's money before they return home and learn the family business. Except instead of being wherever the college in "Back to School" was, this one is in Vermont. The students fain being under stress about academic performance, but it is just acting so daddy can justify to himself the checks he writes for Junior to grow into a well-rounded young man or his little girl to find a good husband without getting pregnant or a venereal disease in the process. In our story, such a nothing college, that has enjoyed a stable client base and relative anonymity, allows its tenured faculty total academic freedom to help cultivate young minds. There motto is "Pay us enough money and your kid won't sound or act like a complete idiot when they inherent the family fortune." Unfortunately or not, Nowhere Vermont College for the Mediocre Offspring of Successful Tradesmen but not rich enough to convince any of the Ivy League schools to let their kid hangout long enough to get a piece of paper that says "Ivy League" somewhere near the word "Awarded." In this case, we have a nobody professor who speaks to nobody students about nothing in particular in exchange for the security of a modest life away from the insanity of the "real world." This nobody professor has a past. He remembers his dreams but he also remembers his principles. He has resigned himself to living out his life speaking to the anonymous. The students seem to enjoy him and he does enjoy them. A quiet life for a man who has learned the hardest of lessons with respect to not being quiet because it violated a rule that he believed in. He will never be quiet and the only place safe for him was someplace that no one of any importance would ever hear him.

POL4350 – Political Absolutes Lecture 1

Professor Bailey Charles

Dr. Charles

We begin this semester together as I have begun so many semesters before. With anticipation. Anticipation of what I might say or what you might learn. I want to do my part by telling you that from this point on, I will be lying to you. Now you can focus on what you might learn. Let's get started.

A long time ago, some words were written in the Greek language about the origins and stages of growth in human consciousness and awareness. The words describe the transition from having no sight - to the images of shadows on a cave wall - to a first-hand experience of the three-dimensional world. There are more words that described the human understanding of the stars in the night sky. Some words were also written that gave human traits to a set of gods that were believed to have influence over how our lives would turn out. These words were the earliest and best intended attempts to have you and I believe that the human condition is something that is separate from some class of being or beings and that we are accountable to a framework of rules as set out by the authors of the words.

Many words have been written about the relationship between the humans and the governing gods. Today we use the word government instead of the word "god." It is not an accident that to say "government" you start to say "god." They are essentially the same thing – creations of the human mind intended to harness the untamed human body. There was a hierarchy and organization to the Greek gods and there is a hierarchy and organization to governments. There are rules to be sure, and the smartest government becomes the most powerful. Finally, there is a subtle insinuation that good will triumph over evil in the end.

The power of the Greek gods was derived from the belief system of the humans. Like Voodoo, the person has to believe in the god in order for the god to have any real control. There are stories about a god that might act like a jerk until the person has no choice but to ask if one of the gods is displeased, but most of the stories just describe the purpose, traits, and tendencies of the various fictional entities. People made money and acquired political power from marketing the merits and making claim to a special relationship with one or more of the gods.

Then the idea of a single god began taking on some popularity and opportunity opened up for the god salesforce to become a government salesforce in order to keep the "donations" flowing. These sales people can just keep doing what they have been doing with a simple single word change. The pitch goes something like, "I am a chosen representative and the single voice for the most just and decent god/government. Render unto me all of your support and I will make sure you reap great blessings from god/government."

When a person gets elected and wants more than what they currently have, the person will say something like, "For too long human beings have been shut out from the riches hoarded by selfish people who worship no god/government and it is time to get them to convert, make amends, or perish."

When a human asks god/government a question, the human is told by a representative of the god/government that god/government has a plan that is too complicated for a mere human to understand and there is no reason to worry because god/government knows what is best for them.

At some point, and it is in the extreme, god/government becomes too sure of itself and its sales force gets a little too pushy. It is at these points that a group of human beings will say to god/government, "Screw you."

What follows the proverbial "Screw you" is very messy. People who might have lived long lives, will not. Beautiful creations will be destroyed. Assets seized will be reassigned. People will choose to endorse a new or different god/government or they will die fighting for the god/government with which they are currently aligned. More words will be written. Some of those words become the history we learn and some of the words become the artificial construct that attempts to govern our lives.

The villains and heroes of history are presented in such a way as to influence the reader to turn towards a certain god/government or turn away from a certain god/government. During the election season, the salespeople use the interchangeable set of choices god/government/party/candidate. The words intended to address the needs of a bureaucracy and human governances will strike a delicate balance between convincing the humans that this god/government is what they needed and not seizing more assets than they can get away with before the humans decide to say "Screw you" again.

There are many ways a human might say "Screw you" to a particular god/government, but the only way that is considered acceptable by civilized society is for humans to become voters that decide which god/government gets the power. The vote. Your vote. What will you be saying this November?

Thank you.

End of Lecture.

Fujiwhara Beach City Council Meeting

Pursuant to Public Notice, Mayor FicChaTwentySeven convened a regular meeting of the City Council in the Council Chamber. Those present were

Mayor FicChaTwentySeven,

Vice-Mayor FicChaTwentySix,

Councilwoman FicChaThirty,

Councilwoman FicChaTwenty,

Councilman FicChaTwoA,

City Attorney FicChaTwentyThree,

And City Manager FicChaTwoBee.

The mayor led a moment of silence and the Pledge of Allegiance.

FicChaTwentySeven The police chief wants to renew an agreement with the county school system for providing resource officers in the schools.

The School Resource Officer Program is the governmental response to the net public fear associated with school shootings. The program was sold to the public as keeping the schools safe. Of the ten published goals of the program, nine of the goals are to establish the role of government in the lives and minds of the students. The last goal is to study better ways to establish the role of government in the lives and minds of the students. It is essentially a tax-funded outreach program to brainwash future generations into the fallacy that government is the answer to their problems. The program's funding source is primarily derived as trickling down from the federal and state levels. From there, the counties dole out to the municipalities. At each level of funding, there are conditions of "shared responsibility" which means that the level below has to do everything the level above mandates, exactly as the level above mandates, and throw some of their own money in the pot for implementation.

FicChaThirty	Please tell me again why we need a police officer in each of our schools? Besides, the county pays the city a total of $62,000 to station an officer at each of the schools within the city limits and it costs the city an additional $23,000 to make up the difference in the real cost of the program and ensure grant compliance. In the interest of good fiscal management, we really need to discuss this.
FicChaTwenty	I move that we renew the agreement.
FicChaTwentySix	I second the motion.
FicChaTwentySeven	A motion has been made and seconded. I call for a vote. I vote "Aye"
FicChaTwentySix	"Aye"
FicChaTwenty	"Aye"
FicChaTwoA	"Aye"
FicChaThirty	Can we talk about this? I want my children to be safe, but is this really the best way to make that happen?
FicChaTwentySeven	I will take that as a "Nay," the "Ayes" have it. The motion carries. The next issue is the application for the Justice Assistance Grant.

The Justice Assistance Grant began at the federal level with conduits to trickle down to the various levels of government. In its current form, various department heads at the various levels of government are to decide how the money is to be spent. All the cities and the county have to agree how the money will be used before anybody gets any money. One can suspect that such a deal is intended to bolster the Republican claim that federal money is distributed to the states to use as they see fit. But what it says, regardless of why it is said, is "I have some gold coins that I will give to you lesser gods to solicit worship from the masses as you see fit. However, before I release a single penny, you must tell me a juicy tale that bolsters my stature." This agreement could have been a "copy and paste" with the types of words that were communicated by the Commintern just after the seizure of power by Lenin … because that is what he had to do in order to get into power in the first place.

FicChaTwentySix	I make a motion that we continue active cooperation and participation in the pursuit of these funds.
FicChaTwenty	I second the motion.
FicChaThirty	To what end? It is a total of $158, 000 to improve the efficiency of criminal prosecution. Criminal prosecutions are a county function. If we arrest someone in Fujiwhara Beach, the county collects them at the time of arrest. Why spend this money?
FicChaTwentySeven	A motion has been made and seconded. I call for a vote. I vote "Aye"
FicChaTwentySix	"Aye"
FicChaTwenty	"Aye"

FicChaTwoA	"Aye"
FicChaThirty	Can we talk about this?
FicChaTwentySix	I will take that as a "Nay," the "Ayes" have it. The motion carries. The next issue is to approve the budget amendment which reflects unrealistically inflated revenue projections at the beginning of the fiscal year.
FicChaThirty	Since the city's founding, annual budget amendments to reflect unrealistically inflated revenue projections has occurred forty-six out of the last fifty years. With computer technology being as advanced as it is, why are we wrong ninety two percent of the time? In the interest of proper government management of tax payers' funds, we need to talk about this.
FicChaTwenty	I make a motion that we adopt the budget amendment as proposed.
FicChaTwentySix	I second the motion.
FicChaTwentySeven	A motion has been made and seconded. I call for a vote. I vote "Aye"
FicChaTwentySix	"Aye"
FicChaTwenty	"Aye"
FicChaTwoA	"Aye"
FicChaThirty	Can we talk about this?

FicChaTwentySeven I will take that as a "Nay," the "Ayes" have it. The motion carries. The next issue is the modification of site planning procedures.

FicChaTwentySix I make a motion that we adopt the ordinance as proposed.

FicChaTwenty I second the motion.

FicChaTwentySeven A motion has been made and seconded. I call for a vote. I vote "Aye"

FicChaTwentySix "Aye"

FicChaTwenty "Aye"

FicChaTwoA "Aye"

FicChaThirty Hold on a minute. The modifications include the requirement to provide documentation from a person certified to make the statement that a specific requirement of a federal regulation is being complied with. In short, the federal government has required that the cities pass laws that force citizens to be compliant with their bright ideas. They are telling us what laws we have to create in order to be able to continue receiving grant money.

FicChaTwentySeven I will take that as a "Nay," the "Ayes" have it. The motion carries. The next issue is vacating some rights of land owners' on canal front property in the city so we can do what we believe is best for all residents of the city with regard to waterfront land use.

FicChaTwenty	I make a motion that vacates the land rights of canal front property owners so we can do what we determine to be best for all involved.
FicChaTwentySix	I second the motion.
FicChaTwentySeven	A motion has been made and seconded. I call for a vote. I vote "Aye"
FicChaTwentySix	"Aye"
FicChaTwenty	"Aye"
FicChaTwoA	"Aye"
FicChaThirty	Why are we doing this? Why are we taking rights away from people? Didn't we all take an oath to defend the Constitution and our local ordinances?
FicChaTwentySeven	I will take that as a "Nay," the "Ayes" have it. The motion carries. The last item in the agenda is the agreement that the Community Redevelopment Agency (CRA) will give us some money to spend on General Fund activities even though those activities are not in our CRA's plan.
FicChaTwenty	I make a motion that we approve the agreement.
FicChaTwentySix	I second the motion.
FicChaTwentySeven	A motion has been made and seconded. I call for a vote. I vote "Aye"

FicChaTwentySix	"Aye"
FicChaTwenty	"Aye"
FicChaTwoA	"Aye"
FicChaThirty	This agreement completely ignores the settlement the city reached with the State Attorney and Joint Legislative Auditing Committee that believed our city was mis-spending CRA funds. Can we discuss this a bit more? I am very uncomfortable with where we are going.
FicChaTwentySeven	I will take that as a "Nay," the "Ayes" have it. The motion carries. That was the last item on the agenda. Meeting adjourned.

The total time of the meeting was less than 45 minutes. It is amazing what you can get done when the seats in the audience are empty and you probably would not listen to citizen comments anyway. In fact, that's exactly why the seats are empty.

In the process of proofreading the text, the pattern became captivating. If you did not have a similar experience, may I suggest going back and re-reading until the pattern emerges for you. This will help you sing along at the next meeting. What is cool about this group is that you could skip a few meetings and jump right in when the chorus comes along. The meetings are interesting in the sense of the nuanced and couched issues that seem to be disconnected solos at first, but start assuming some thematic qualities that lead the reader towards a grand finale.

Election Day minus 87 days

Weather Report Fujiwhara Beach, FL

Actual	Avg.	Record	
Mean Temperature	84 °F		
Max Temperature	87 °F	85 °F	91 °F (2011)
Min Temperature	80 °F	74 °F	71 °F (2003)
Dew Point	71 °F		
Average Humidity	64		
Maximum Humidity	77		
Minimum Humidity	58		
Precipitation	0.00 in		
Sea Level Pressure	30.07 in		
Wind Speed	10 mph (SE)		
Max Wind Speed	16 mph		
Max Gust Speed	-		
Visibility	10 miles		
Events	None		

That Saturday Morning

Most Saturday mornings for the past several months, TGTDTT and MickBill get together for breakfast at a local diner in Fujiwhara Beach that MickBill likes. It began at the request of TGTDTT because he saw MickBill as a potential example of what to expect if he were to make the same kinds of decisions that MickBill has made. On the air during his daily morning radio show, MickBill speaks of a colorful past before he became a local radio celebrity. When TGTDTT ran the data provided courtesy of the MickBill radio talk show through his "What can I learn from this person?" filter, the output was insight into perseverance.

There are people who talk the talk, and then there are people who deal with a number of major course shifts in their lives and just seem to keep on going. Day after day, for three hours a day, MickBill puts himself out there to capture the attention of the audience so that sponsors will purchase air time. If you were to ask TGTDTT who MickBill was, he would probably respond that MickBill is his friend. It wasn't always like that, but MickBill's sincerity in everything he does deserves respect and having TGTDTT's respect is a major step towards a lasting friendship.

MickBill is quite aware of the merits associated with surrendering his life to a higher power but he would rather not surrender any aspect of his life to the control of government. It is because MickBill appreciates the karmic downsides to any effort to relinquish him of his responsibilities to himself, his family, his friends, and somewhere on the list includes the good ole "You Ess of Aye." So his show is mostly about local government activity with some mention of the broader world as he deems appropriate. He gets a lot of guests, especially during the election season.

MickBill is also an institutional man in the sense he was, among other things, a member of the National Guard, a former policeman, and a baseball umpire. So to be fair, MickBill wants every government program cut that does not adversely affect the government programs he supports. The good news is that he knows this about himself so he caveats a lot of what he says on the radio in order to keep any stone throwers on the bench and out of the game.

The people who call in to his show cover the entire range of mental health from emotionally troubled people to elected officials (which are not always different people). Rarely does a caller ever come after MickBill over the air. There was one occasion in which a regular caller who went off his medication ended up being terminated by sheriff's deputies with just cause on the courthouse lawn. The caller used to make up different names when he called in because he knows MickBill limits the frequency an individual may be on the air. When MickBill caught on, the caller got his own theme song that would play to announce the caller's arrival or departure. When news of the termination reached MickBill, his next show contained a segment that said a respectful "Farewell," played the chosen theme song in his memory, and then publically retired the song from his play list.

It is that kind of stuff like that keeps TGTDTT coming to these Saturday morning breakfasts. MickBill is tapped into the system at all levels. He had a history with the person on the receiving end of the termination and a personal and professional relationship with the person who gave the order to terminate. TGTDTT could see MickBill make the transitions that people go through when something pretty traumatic happens. When it came time for his voice to be heard, MickBill said the right thing and then moved on. TGTDTT remembers the caller but never knew about the song.

MickBill	(typing into his camouflage cased iPhone) Let me just finish this email real quick.
TGTDTT	No problem.

The regular Saturday thing has come to include a regular table, a regular waitress, and a regular drink order. MickBill usually has a biscuit, bacon, and fruit. TGTDTT has whatever Holly and her colleagues decide to serve him that day.

MickBill	So how you been?
TGTDTT	I was recently reading this biography on Lenin.
MickBill	John?
TGTDTT	No. The other one.
MickBill	Those glasses you wear make you kind of look like John.
TGTDTT	No. (Pause) The book was written by a retired Russian general who at one point was in charge of the administration and cleanup of documents that had been classified as secret or above during Lenin and Stalin's reign. Every minute piece of paper generated by the Russian government was considered a state secret. Every piece of information concerning the government's control of the country's finances was considered a state secret of the highest order. Only the select few had knowledge of how much money was in the control of government and how that money was being spent.
MickBill	I would expect that.

TGDTT — The point of this book was to take the reader through the events that would create a Lenin and a government publically committed to the rights of the workers by a detailed accounting of internal memos written by Lenin, Trotsky, Stalin, and presenting the official documents concerning who got exiled, who got executed, who got relocated, and who got what. From very early in Lenin's life, he decided that he was going to get his and he was going to get even and eventually, he would only get more if the committee thought he should get it. Lenin had no boundaries in terms of his thoughts, words, or deeds as to what he was willing to do to make sure his master plan was put into effect.

MickBill — What is your point?

TGTDTT — Recently people have demonstrated a concern for the influence that Saul Alinsky has had on some of our high-ranking elected officials, including some local ones. My thesis is that Saul Alinsky got it from Lenin.

Today TGTDTT was served biscuits with sausage gravy, two eggs over easy, and some fruit. MickBill had the usual.

MickBill — I know you have a point, I just don't know what it could possibly be.

TGTDTT — At the root of the rise of a dictatorship are entirely too many people who think they got it bad, and that doing what the voice tells them to do will make it better. It never occurs to them that the voice is lying to them. The voice is saying "You are in pain, I know what your pain is and I can take it away if you vote for me." How can people not understand that no one can keep that promise no matter how hard they might try, even if they wanted to in the first place?

MickBill — Now you're sounding like you are going after the pharmaceutical industry. Besides, Lenin was never actually elected to anything.

TGTDTT — A vote is a vote is a vote. Whether it is cast at the polling place or in a small back room somewhere, I promise you that Lenin was elected to the position he held and was given the power to write the words that he wrote which caused the actions that occurred. Once that power was granted, Lenin went on a jihad to secure his grasp. It took his entire lifetime, but he pulled it off just the same.

MickBill — So what are you suggesting?

TGTDTT — I am suggesting that you and I are here right now, and someplace else there is someone who is writing words in which you and I end up exiled, executed, or relocated.

MickBill — Have you been listening to Jesse Ventura?

TGTDTT — I am not listening to anybody. You and I both have appreciation for grand plans.

The reason that you and I have breakfast every Saturday morning is neither of us know what our grand plan is. The people who run for office at the lower levels have some plan, but not a grand plan. At the highest levels of government there is a small group of people who are not elected but have a grand plan and they implement that plan through the people who get elected to office. Somewhere out there is a document that contains the words government would use to justify seizing all of our assets and incarcerate or re-educate the dissenters and someone is devoting their entire life to being able to sign it and say it is a law.

MickBill

I am pretty sure FicChaTwenty has already drafted such a document and is just waiting for the right time to have the Fujiwhara Beach City Council vote to approve it.

TGTDTT

I think the reason that I am thinking the things I am thinking is because when I am not listening to talk radio, I am reading books about the people who tried to conquer the world and the people who stopped them from doing it. My experience with the Fujiwhara Beach City Council was my first exposure to people who believe they know what is best for me and that I need to sit down, shut up, and be thankful that they are there. FicChaTen tried to change that, but look what happened to him. He is doing what he can to keep the fight going, but it is from the sidelines and it seems from a higher level maybe. FicChaTen seems excited about one of the candidates for County Commissioner District 4, but there are seven or eight people running for that seat that are all registered Republicans, even though only one or two down deep really are. Somewhere, someplace, right now people are strategizing on which person to support, and how best to support them, so that their grand plan is being serviced.

MickBill Is that what you and I are doing right now?

TGTDTT We are just two guys having breakfast.

Election Day minus 86 days

Weather Report where the Committee meets

Actual	Avg.	Record	
Mean Temperature	80 °F	79 °F	
Max Temperature	84 °F	87 °F	98 °F (1943)
Min Temperature	75 °F	71 °F	55 °F (1919)
Dew Point	66 °F		
Average Humidity	61		
Maximum Humidity	76		
Minimum Humidity	46		
Precipitation	0.01 in	0.09 in	1.64 (1878)
Sea Level Pressure	30.04 in		
Wind Speed	7 mph (WNW)		
Max Wind Speed	12 mph		
Max Gust Speed	16 mph		
Visibility	10 miles		
Events	Rain		

Homeland Security Summary to Committee

Never forget that the United States of America exists because the government of the United States of America is recognized by the governments of the states that are united and governments of other states that are not united with us. Thus is the charter of Homeland Security. There is an equation that has been programmed into a computer that is under the control of Government of the United States of America Department of Homeland security that yields a numerical answer to the budgetary requirements to ensure the continuity of the government. Within their purview are all potential threats, foreign and domestic. Justification for that number is an aggregation of individual threat points. Homeland Security developed a five axis system by which the security of government could be communicated based on the principal points of potential attack. They also developed a standard language that changes as conditions change. Each of the statements in the summary is computer generated and tailored to speak to the intent of the committee that will act on it.

- Population deemed subversive to government is within current guidelines if a Phase 1 lockdown were required.

- Nine out of ten voters align themselves with the current two party electoral system.

- None of the recognized international governments have committed resources to directly threaten the government.

- Threats of force to government are numerous and small. Their randomness and short lifespan render them harmless in the long run.

- The single biggest threat to government is the upcoming nationwide election. It is possible, but not likely, that independent candidates could replace party-affiliated candidates in many critical offices.

Committee Meeting

A rise in the noise floor among the masses has been detected.

Meeting of the members of the Committee. No Names. No Observers. They refer to each other by a number - One, Two, Three, Four and Five. The appointment to the committee is a life term. Their membership on the committee is never discussed. Committee members do not acknowledge each other as Committee members except in the privacy of the meeting when all five are present. The five committee members have taken a solemn oath to hold the Sabbath Day in the service of that elusive dream that has been passed on from generation to generation for almost four hundred hears. Each member knows that their selection is not an offer that can be refused and that being replaced is just a matter of time. It is understood that the fate of the predecessor is never discussed. The replacement is never welcomed. Once you are told where to report so that you will sit in the chair that has been sat in for just one century shy of half a millennium, you are in the chair. Your entire life has prepared you for sitting in the chair and the job is too important to demean it with sentimentality of any sort. These five people know who they are and why they exist. Without them, anarchy would consume the land.

One	I sense a rise in the noise floor. It could be random, but I am not sure.
Two	Abraham Lincoln and Bill Clinton were the results of independent candidates entering the race.
Five	They don't count. The winners in both those races were one of the big two. No congressmen since the first continental congress and no president since George

Washington has ever been elected to office without being a standard bearer for some organized group of people.

Three — What is your point?

Four — Five's point is that we don't have to worry. Somehow, somewhere there is somebody who makes promises to the voters that the voters want kept. We will eventually own whoever gets elected. But One is also right that every now and then a person comes along that convinces others that their lives would be better without the government they currently have. Depending on how we handle that person will determine how many other people have to die.

Three — What are you suggesting?

One — I am suggesting that we become a little more in tune with the weather. A storm could care less whether you know about it or not. If we could prevent the right moth from flying counterclockwise around a particular tree, the storm would never form in the first place.

Three — I am to understand the balance of power will remain in the hands of those beholden to the committee. Who cares about the storm?

Four — One is suggesting that the committee is being threatened and our survival depends on being able to weather it out or find the source and stop it from ever occurring. One's concern is that the threat he senses could be something the committee cannot weather. What all of you seem to accept is that our purpose is to be in total control and this threat will never go away. The power of this perceived threat is much greater than any power we can ever understand or control. It seems to me that it is only a matter of time, and our role is try to postpone the inevitable.

Five — That is so like you. Your attitude is so fatalistic.

Four — I know which way the water will flow but cannot say for certain where it will end up. The reason it flows is predetermined and there is nothing I can do about that. Who am I to say that the flowing of water is a bad thing when it is the result of a divine truth? When a dam breaks and floods a town, killing many people, I ask why people would live at the base of a dam. The reason they live at the base of a dam is because they either did not know they live at the base of a dam or it is because we told them it was safe. We would never say such things if we thought the flood would reach us. What if we are the ones now living under a dam? The dam that we built.

Election Day minus 83 days

Weather Report Northfield, VT

Actual	Avg.	Record	
Mean Temperature	63 °F	66 °F	
Max Temperature	71 °F	77 °F	91 °F (1988)
Min Temperature	54 °F	54 °F	39 °F (1950)
Dew Point	58 °F		
Average Humidity	87		
Maximum Humidity	100		
Minimum Humidity	73		
Precipitation	0.16 in	0.13 in	1.76 (1997)
Sea Level Pressure	29.84 in		
Wind Speed	5 mph (South)		
Max Wind Speed	17 mph		
Max Gust Speed	22 mph		
Visibility	6 miles		
Events	Fog, Rain		

The Dr. Charles Lectures - Two to the Fifth

POL4350 – Political Absolutes Lecture 2

Professor Bailey Charles

Dr. Charles

Just as I lied to you last week, I am going to lie to you some more.

I attended a three day "leadership summit" in Las Vegas and one of the speakers made reference to a study that indicated that the human mind, at its peak performance level, is able to process up to five binary variables. Stress causes the introduction of cortisone which incrementally reduces the number of variables we can simultaneously process. Under maximum stress, the fight or flight choice, is the universally accepted final variable to be considered.

Five variables, five senses, five fingers, five toes, five business days in a calendar, Earth week, five players on a basketball team. All these fives. Five is a prime number and is considered great if you are a hotel, or horrible if you are an aspiring model.

Five binary variables means that at any time, there are thirty-two possible outcomes to be considered. As our cognitive capacity is diminished, the reduction is first to sixteen, then eight, then four, then two, then one and will remain at one until death.

Unless something happens that reduces the cortisone in our bloodstream. The less cortisone in our bloodstream, the more choices we have.

Quoting a study that I just made up because it supports my world view is that endorphins are the chemical intended to lower cortisone levels. I don't know if endorphins dissolve cortisone or cause it to run back to its hole or what, but if it were true, it would explain a great deal knowing that endorphins are maximized when a person is in a joyous state. In the world of spatial mechanics, the joyous state seems a pretty good distance away from a stressful state. So it seems that people in a joyous state have more choices than a person in a stressful state.

Voting for a candidate carries the same mathematical properties as the single variable processing of the human mind. Does the mind recognize the situation in the same manner as a fight or flight choice? It would make sense if we found out that the physiological responses were the same. But knowing this to be true would mark the point in time at which the demise of the human race may be predicted. Whether it is true or not, the industry of politics is to guide or lead the unruly herd of voters through the various cattle shoots so they come out the other end as the meat a particular candidate could count on eating as a sausage of contributions and influence.

The role of the political parties is to round up the unregistered and get them registered to the party that caught them.

A young person who has just ventured out on their own after eighteen years filled with love, security, and restrictions that only parents can provide, will enter the fray with some conditioned notion as to their single biggest fear. Into their life comes a voice that says "It is okay. I love you. Now that you are an adult, I am the one to turn to in times of need. I will treat you with the respect I believe you deserve. I will make sure you have everything you need, just like your parents did. Except there is no curfew. You can do pretty much anything you want to do. In fact, you don't even need to go to church if you would rather not. All I need from you is your vote. If you really want to help me make the world of your dreams, then I would be happy to take whatever money you can spare and/or you can volunteer on my campaign."

The reason such a person might be persuaded by such a voice is that they believe it is possible for another person to be responsible but not in control at the same time. The only way for me to be totally responsible for how something turns out is to be in total control of what and how things are being done. In the case of the needs of another person, it is impossible to be totally responsible for another person. The voice is offering something that doesn't exist. If the voice can influence your decisions at the most base level, then you will choose to believe that the control government asserts is acceptable. If you are like most people, you have thresholds of tolerance. The challenge of the voice is to keep you believing that more work needs to be done and that you are still in need of care. Care that only government can provide.

Thank you.

End of Lecture

Election Day minus 80 days

Weather Report Fujiwhara Beach, FL

Actual	Avg.	Record	
Mean Temperature	82 °F		
Max Temperature	86 °F	85 °F	89 °F (2002)
Min Temperature	77 °F	75 °F	71 °F (2008)
Dew Point	74 °F		
Average Humidity	77		
Maximum Humidity	87		
Minimum Humidity	66		
Precipitation	0.00 in		
Sea Level Pressure	30.05 in		
Wind Speed	7 mph (SSE)		
Max Wind Speed	13 mph		
Max Gust Speed	-		
Visibility	10 miles		
Events	None		

That Saturday Morning

How are the sounds of a parent trying to quiet a shrieking child or a dog owner yelling at the unruly dog they brought to the diner with them considered behavior one would intentionally expose to the general public? These were two of the small sacrifices that TGTDTT chose to make so that MickBill could enjoy an after breakfast mentholated nicotine inhaler treatment which is prohibited by law inside a public building. This morning, the crowd noise seemed more noticeable. TGTDTT had gotten to the diner early so that he could sit for a quiet moment reading one of the books he brought with him. So much for the quiet.

MickBill	I brought a guest with me. ShugaJoel meet TGTDTT.
ShugaJoel	I heard a lot about you and have been looking forward to meeting you one day.
TGTDTT	I was young and needed the money. I don't do that anymore.
ShugaJoel	Excuse me?
MickBill	What are you reading?
TGTDTT	It is called "The Truth About Muhammad."
MickBill	Anything worth talking about?
TGTDTT	If I were to make any decisions about my view of the world based on what I have read so far, the choice is to kill myself or kill everyone who is even remotely associated with radical Islam. If I chose the latter, I would then end up having to kill

everyone even remotely associated with Islam. Because if I don't kill them for being Muslim, they will kill me because I am not.

Holly took ShugaJoel's drink order which gave him a much desired opportunity to be a part of the conversation. Without getting into specifics, TGTDTT began to wonder why ShugaJoel would have heard anything about TGTDTT, and if he had, why ShugaJoel would end up wanting to have breakfast with TGTDTT.

TGTDTT — Excuse me, but aren't you the reason FicChaTwelve ran for Fujiwhara Beach City Council two years ago?

ShugaJoel — I was seriously considering running at the time but decided not to for health reasons.

TGTDTT — I am not passing judgment. It just helps to see more of the picture. I was one of the people who stepped in with support after FicChaTwelve told me he had decided to run. He got slaughtered on Election Day. I was proud to be one of the few people who weren't family he wanted to share a drink with that night. FicChaTwelve fought the good fight in an honorable way. But the voters of Fujiwhara Beach saw things differently. They wanted the safety of the old way of doing things before FicChaTen and company began doing crazy things like looking for more efficient ways to run the government, cutting the budget and taxes, and increasing the city's reserve funds.

ShugaJoel — I know I could have gotten more votes than FicChaTwenty. I grew up here my entire

	life. Went to Fujiwhara Beach High School. I was also one of the assistant varsity football coaches.
MickBill	Sorry about that (getting off the phone). What were you two talking about?
TGTDTT	Is the McDermant story true?
MickBill	It is indeed.
TGTDTT	I am perceiving rumblings that the investigation of her husband was called for by an impure spirit.
MickBill	People can think what they want. The search warrant was real. The arrest warrant was real. The mug shots are real. And the indictment will be real.
TGTDTT	The posting I was forwarded was the first thing I had ever read from her. It was off the charts, I could not imagine it was real.
ShugaJoel	I know Liza McDermant and that posting sounded exactly like her.
TGTDTT	She drops out of the race for County Commission District 4. That leaves seven.
MickBill	Eight.
TGTDTT	I know FicChaTen's choice is your choice too. How's he doing?

MickBill	He is doing well. He got in the race early and has been systematically meeting all of the milestones with respect to petition signatures, canvassing early, absentee, and super voters.
TGTDTT	How can there be eight registered Republicans challenging for the same seat?
MickBill	You are looking at this all wrong. A robust primary is a good thing. At least it is for my show.
TGTDTT	Do you believe the candidates are keeping a media trail that they use for post-game analysis?
MickBill	I see where you are going with this and I think you are being overly cynical.

A brief indulgence to make a point.

Producer — Cue Music

Your Host — Ladies and Gentlemen, or more appropriately, registered Republicans in Mosquito County, Florida District 4, I bring to you a selection of the best your district has to offer. Most of the people you are about to meet actually live in your district right now. But rest assured, they all promise to buy or rent in the district during their term in office if they get elected.

Now before you meet them individually, I want to go ahead and tell you some more that all of the candidates promise to do if they are elected.

They are going fight for your rights. Government will be no larger and no smaller than it has to be to keep you safe and secure.

Well, it looks like we have run out of time, but remember that voting for a Republican in the primary is just like selecting which burger joint you want to eat at for lunch. But voting Republican in the general election means choosing liberty over servitude.

Producer — Cue Music

Producer — And we're out.

Election Day minus 79 days

Weather Report where the Committee meets

Actual	Avg.	Record	
Mean Temperature	72 °F	78 °F	
Max Temperature	81 °F	87 °F	105 °F (1997)
Min Temperature	63 °F	70 °F	51 °F (1902)
Dew Point	57 °F		
Average Humidity	62		
Maximum Humidity	84		
Minimum Humidity	39		
Precipitation	0.00 in	0.09 in	2.39 (1879)
Sea Level Pressure	30.24 in		
Wind Speed	8 mph (ENE)		
Max Wind Speed	16 mph		
Max Gust Speed	21 mph		
Visibility	10 miles		
Events	None		

Homeland Security Summary to Committee

- Population deemed subversive to government remains within current guidelines if a Phase 1 lockdown were required.

- Eighty seven out of one hundred voters align themselves with the current two party electoral system.

- The nationalization of industries abroad have exposed weaknesses in the control of sensitive information transmitted over the air or through a network.

- Threats of force to government are numerous. The extent of the threats is unknown.

- The single biggest threat to government is the upcoming nationwide election. It is possible, but not likely that independent candidates could replace party affiliated candidates in many critical offices.

Committee Meeting

A low pressure area has been detected.

Five	The money is slowing. Walking backwards in the data trail shows a distribution that is relatively uniform. Demographically, the walk-aways are a cross section of the population with only a slight bias towards the younger generation.
One	We have identified the low pressure area.
Five	There's more.
One	I would hope so.
Five	The common link was found by looking at internet activity and doing some serious cross correlation. All of these people made their support known through data transactions processed on the web. Further analysis showed that their withdrawal of support from the recognized political parties was redirected towards candidates with no party affiliation. They are all registered Independents with severe libertarian streaks.
Three	How many?
Five	Following the data using the algorithm that identified the current trend, Homeland Security reports about thirteen percent.

Two	To be clear, we can say with mathematical certainty that thirteen percent of the registered voters all did the same thing and continue to do the exact same thing?
Five	The overall binding element were identical views of a video series posted on the YouTube website.
Four	The Dr. Charles Lectures.
Two	It starts now. But we have to be sure.
One	How much more certainty do you want? I am glad you were not on the committee when we were discussing whether or not to go to the moon.
Four	I find myself thinking of track five of disc one of the musical soundtrack of Andrew Lloyd Webber's "Jesus Christ Superstar." We all know how this is going to play out.

Election Day minus 76 days

Weather Report Northfield, VT

Actual	Avg.	Record	
Mean Temperature	67 °F	65 °F	
Max Temperature	80 °F	77 °F	87 °F (1955)
Min Temperature	53 °F	53 °F	39 °F (1953)
Dew Point	56 °F		
Average Humidity	73		
Maximum Humidity	100		
Minimum Humidity	45		
Precipitation	0.00 in	0.12 in	1.09 (2006)
Sea Level Pressure	30.11 in		
Wind Speed	3 mph (WNW)		
Max Wind Speed	10 mph		
Max Gust Speed	15 mph		
Visibility	4 miles		
Events	Fog		

The Dr. Charles Lectures - A Truly Free Market

POL4350 – Political Absolutes Lecture 3

Professor Bailey Charles

Dr. Charles

Good afternoon. I want you to know, as I have said many times before, that I am lying to you, have been lying to you, and will continue to lie to you so that my reality inches closer to my world view. I will even lie about what my world view is if it helps my cause. As your teacher, it is my sincerest wish that you will see through my lies to something closer to the truth. Now let's get down to business.

The cost of goods and services is driven by real influences of needing to attract talent and arbitrary influences imposed by governments. At the time of this nation's founding, the private sector was the overwhelming guiding force as to the cost of goods and services and the government's role was limited to the role of charging fees for permits and licenses and enforcing a very small set of laws. In the beginning of this nation, things were as I dream they might be once again.

Each business owner would have the right to run their business as they saw fit.

One could argue that government and unions bring order to the free-flow of commerce and that everyone wins when both are involved. The counter argument would include a history lesson that the "socialization" of anything ruins the very thing it socialized. But the real argument lies in the collective threshold for graft.

Since the writing of the Ten Commandments, the majority of the laws passed by government have a revenue component that feeds into the budget process of the people voting for the law. There is not a single heavily unionized industry in the United States that has thrived in the last century without the majority support of government contracts or laws that mandate the use of their services.

The good news is that it has been this way since the beginning of recorded history. It did not become efficient until money was invented and people started writing stuff down. Money was a good shorthand way of assessing security requirements. A person could look at a number and decide whether they need a better hiding place or more guards. They could also calculate their profit if they spent some of their own money to pay some people to take someone else's money.

The price of celery in the produce department of the grocery store is as high as it can possibly be and I will still buy it. The same thing is true of everything I buy. It is also true of everything that everyone buys. When people won't pay the asking price, the seller will lower the price until someone buys. Money has made this reality possible. It would not be possible for governments and unions to have any real impact if we were on the barter system where nothing had a common value. A chicken might be more valuable to one person than it is to another.

If chickens became accepted as standard currency, people would be raising some chickens on their own and looking for ways to get some of your chickens. Governments would form and pass laws that say if you want to live here, you have to give us some chickens. Neighborhood groups would form to "protect the neighborhood" in exchange for regular payments of chickens. If you wanted to sell your lawn mowing business, the price would be in chickens. If I help you sell your lawn mowing business, you will give me some chickens.

By creating a common framework and language to facilitate the exchange of goods and services, people can profit from the mere knowledge of the language and absolutely no knowledge of the goods and services. There is an historical trend towards global consolidation of the financial system. From time to time an international decision is made that moves all the different countries closer together in some way.

Is this the beginning of a "Tower of Babble" thing coming to the surface regarding the establishment of a single common language? And the "Tower of Babble" story is an example of a really big psychic solar flare. There is also historical precedent for the natural aggregation of stuff until it became a place that creates a new form of life. The invention of money has already given birth to the professional political operative which is a life form all unto itself.

On a more personal level, there are times when I would rather not have to spend as much money as I am spending for the things I want. But I ask myself if the item I am seeking will bring me the same or more inner peace than the money in my pocket. My answer is always the same. If I have to ask the question, I don't need the thing. If I don't need the thing, why am I going to buy it?

Those who think that I do not buy things based on what I just said are wrong. I do buy things. But if I find myself affected by price, then I don't buy it. That is a free market. Everything I buy that such a question is moot at best, I just do what I have to do to make sure I can buy it. The way I do that is trust that God will provide me all that I need by only buying the things that I believe God wants me to have, which includes the occasional glass of Knob Creek Bourbon.

I thank you for your time.

End of Lecture

Proceeding towards the rear of the auditorium backstage area to the exit door, down a short alley and then to the faculty dorm where Dr. Charles had a two room suite with private bath on the top floor. One of the rooms is the bedroom, the other is a living/library/office room filled with books and papers with a small clerks' desk with chair, some comfortable reading chairs, and a foot stool. Bailey Charles unlocked the door as he always did. Flipped the light switch like he always did. But the light connected to the switch did not turn on like it always had. A desk lamp on the clerk's desk did come on. The lamp shined just enough light to make out that a person was sitting in one of the reading chairs.

Dr. Charles	May I help you?
Stranger	You already are.
Dr. Charles	I see.
Stranger	I just came by to let you know the committee has identified you as a potential monument candidate.
Dr. Charles	I am a nobody with no agenda. I make it clear that I am not to be taken seriously.
Stranger	You know how this works. What did you think was going to happen? Besides, it is not your choice. What is your choice is how you deal with what I have just told you.

Fujiwhara Beach City Council Meeting

Pursuant to Public Notice, Mayor FicChaTwentySeven convened a regular meeting of the City Council in the Council Chamber. Those present were

```
Mayor FicChaTwentySeven,

Vice-Mayor FicChaTwentySix,

Councilwoman FicChaThirty,

Councilwoman FicChaTwenty,

Councilman FicChaTwoA,

City Attorney FicChaTwentyThree,

And City Manager FicChaTwoBee.
```

The mayor led a moment of silence and the Pledge of Allegiance.

FicChaTwentySeven	You all know why we are here.
FicChaTwenty	I make a motion that we approve the budget as submitted.
FicChaTwentySix	I second the motion.
FicChaTwentySeven	A motion has been made and seconded. I call for a vote. I vote "Aye"
FicChaTwentySix	"Aye"
FicChaTwenty	"Aye"
FicChaTwoA	"Aye"

FicChaThirty	Hold on just a second. I have questions about some of the revenue forecasts.
FicChaTwentySeven	I will take that as a "Nay," the "Ayes" have it. The motion carries. That was the only item on the agenda. Meeting adjourned.

Ladies and gentlemen, this was a record in the history of Fujiwhara Beach. Gavel to gavel coverage of the only publically recorded discussion of the budget by our elected officials in less than seven minutes.

This was the first time a budget was submitted with a slogan, which was "Better living in Fujiwhara Beach starts with our employees." In many ways, it was the best published accounting of the deal to be made with the voting public, but at the same time it wreaked of propaganda. "Here are the reasons we love you more than anyone else so you need to feel good about the money we are taking from you this year." With that being said, many of the expenditures are perfectly justifiable if you think that is what government should be doing for you. Growing numbers of us are asking government to do more, and it is doing more. The people we have elected to do the things we have asked government to do prove they are doing more by authorizing funding for various "feel good" projects. These projects are submitted by "professional" municipal managers, who are usually steeped in the progressive tradition of growing their own rice bowls.

The city's budget was a sales pitch and four members of the Fujiwhara Beach City Council were sold. But don't think it was love at first sight, because they didn't really even look at it beyond analyzing whether the picture of the City Council would be a good picture to the citizens who wanted to be "kept" by their government.

Election Day minus 73 days

Weather Report Fujiwhara Beach, FL

Actual	Avg.	Record	
Mean Temperature	84 °F		
Max Temperature	86 °F	85 °F	93 °F (2010)
Min Temperature	81 °F	75 °F	73 °F (1997)
Dew Point	74 °F		
Average Humidity	74		
Maximum Humidity	82		
Minimum Humidity	62		
Precipitation	0.00 in		
Sea Level Pressure	30.03 in		
Wind Speed	9 mph (ESE)		
Max Wind Speed	18 mph		
Max Gust Speed	-		
Visibility	10 miles		
Events	None		

That Saturday Morning

TGTDTT	Did you catch Professor Charles' webcast for this week?
MickBill	Why do you listen to that guy?
TGTDTT	Why do you care? It doesn't steal from the quality time I spend listening to your dulcet tones from six to nine in the morning every weekday.
MickBill	I guess I would be concerned if you were asking me about the alien encounter show. But you have to admit that Professor Charles is a little over the top for a political lawyer.
TGTDTT	First of all, his Ph.D. is in Physics, he is a tenured college professor at a college that remembers the good old days when the best source of truth comes from a person who has nothing to lose and very little to gain. Sure there are opportunities for corruption, but this is a guy who lives in the faculty dorm and eats in the faculty dining room. The only time he travels is to see his brother in Maine and he drives a well-used and abused '96 Camaro Z28. It is almost as if his simple and limited travels have allowed his mind to settle so that he can see better. His lectures are just what he does. His books and published writings meet the minimum requirements of the university, but nothing more and nothing that feeds revenues into any account he controls.

Maybe he protest a bit too much, but he begins every lecture by telling you that he is about to lie to you but that the lies he tells might help others find the truth. It is almost as if his lectures are monologues that an actor gives on stage. He gives one lecture a week. The rest of the time he holds office hours or does his research and professional writing. He doesn't do interviews and the only video or audio of him is what the students take and upload to the web. I was one of five million people to view his most recent post.

MickBill — How do you know so much about him?

TGTDTT — He is a friend of mine.

MickBill — That is impressive. But he could never make it in the mainstream.

TGTDTT — Why do you do that?

MickBill — Do what?

TGTDTT — Fall victim to the compulsion to assert an opinion that is neither required nor relevant. You are not on the air right now and you don't need to fill every available moment with potential sound bites.

MickBill — I don't?

TGTDTT — What you might want to check out is the ripple effect of his weekly lectures. Most of the time I can't really even remember what he was talking about, but I came away understanding something that seemed good to know. I did some digging around and found several blogs and chat rooms that mention "The Dr. Charles Lectures" and the influence those lectures might be having on the voters.

MickBill — What kind of influence?

TGTDTT — Since his lectures have been posted to the web, some twelve million views are recorded. The view counts divided by the calculated number of voters seems to forecast the percentage of voters an independent candidate or candidates may come to expect.

MickBill — Shut up.

TGTDTT — A case could be made that the two party political system would become a relic of the past if the number of views for his lectures hits the hundred million view mark. If that happens, the general election becomes an all-out free for all.

MickBill — So what do you suggest you or I do?

TGTDTT — I suggest we finish eating our breakfast and get on with living our lives.

Election Day minus 72 days

Weather Report where the Committee meets

Actual	Avg.	Record	
Mean Temperature	75 °F	77 °F	
Max Temperature	85 °F	86 °F	98 °F (1968)
Min Temperature	64 °F	69 °F	49 °F (1890)
Dew Point	58 °F		
Average Humidity	62		
Maximum Humidity	87		
Minimum Humidity	37		
Precipitation	0.00 in	0.09 in	3.47 (1967)
Sea Level Pressure	30.25 in		
Wind Speed	7 mph (NE)		
Max Wind Speed	13 mph		
Max Gust Speed	16 mph		
Visibility	10 miles		
Events	None		

Homeland Security Summary to Committee

- Population deemed subversive to government remains within current guidelines if a Phase 1 lockdown were required.
- Eighty six out of one hundred voters align themselves with the current two party electoral system.
- The nationalization of industries abroad have exposed weaknesses in the control of sensitive information transmitted over the air or through a network.
- Threats of force to government are numerous. The extent of the threats is unknown.
- The single biggest threat to government is the upcoming nationwide election. It is possible, but not likely that independent candidates could replace party affiliated candidates in many critical offices.

Committee Meeting

A seed of revolution has been discovered.

One	The awareness of the voting public continues to grow. As each day passes, their immunity to our spells and chants gets stronger. I see a time in the not-too-distant future where we will have no control over them at all.
Two	Revolutions come and go, but we remain. This awareness you speak of does not exist in my operational area. Governmental controls on all facets of telecommunications, including satellite communications, keeps the problem at a very manageable level.
Three	This college professor is getting all the credit. Or are we giving him credit?
One	Both. When references to his lectures began to appear in the postings of internet blogs we deem subversive, we saw why he was getting the credit and at the same time, making sure he gets credit for other things as well. He is a difficult political adversary because he truly has no political ambition and has no desire for fame or fortune.
Four	He knows that we are prepared to honor him in death.
Five	No. This one is too smart. We sent a messenger and the professor saw right through

our offer. He knows we plan to destroy him if he becomes a bigger problem.

Three — Who did you send?

Five — I sent my nephew.

Two — No wonder the message got screwed up in delivery. You know that your sister's kid has no appreciation for nuance.

Five — Well it turns out that my nephew was one of the professor's fans. He felt he owed it to him to make sure he understood the truth without actually betraying any confidences.

One — Your nephew put his loyalty to a subversive above his loyalty to this committee and its members ... especially a member who happens to be a close relative. I want him presented to this committee immediately.

Five — You think you want that, but you really don't. Besides, all of your questions would go unanswered and your charges would fall on deaf ears.

Two — How is your sister managing?

Five — She put up a good show as the wounded mother. When she realized that no one cared because it was the kid's fault, she got a little angry. When she got a visit from one of Three's people, she settled right down.

One — So what do we do about the professor?

Four

There is nothing we can do that will help us. Tampering with the professor in any way will hurt us. Did any of you stop to think if this is a good thing?

Two

Look, you're new here. Some of us have been on the committee for a long time and all of us were raised from birth to be on this committee. The people's reaction to the professor's lectures is to turn away from all forms of government and to elect independent candidates who seek to dismantle government. The reason we are still here is that no committee member can hold public office. Because we protected the two political parties, the two political parties protected the committee. If the elected officials owe nothing to the political parties, then they owe nothing to us. We are vulnerable and it cannot be accepted that we remain vulnerable.

Three

It is just one professor.

Two

The last time an unconventional teacher got the public's attention, our predecessors ordered him to be put to death and the people started a religion. It was hard enough to negotiate a revenue sharing agreement with the major religions we have now, I don't want to go through it again. Besides, what if the religion that gets started is the one that converts all of the other religions. Right now, we know that the big three are too tied to the riches of this world to ever unite. I believe those are the three we get. If we handle this professor wrong and another religion gets started, I am betting it will be the one that puts an end to the committee. The professor needs to drive his very old and very used '96 Camaro Z28 very fast on a very wet and very foggy road.

Election Day minus 69 days

Weather Report Northfield, VT

Actual	Avg.	Record	
Mean Temperature	71 °F	64 °F	
Max Temperature	80 °F	75 °F	91 °F (1952)
Min Temperature	62 °F	52 °F	36 °F (1954)
Dew Point	65 °F		
Average Humidity	81		
Maximum Humidity	100		
Minimum Humidity	62		
Precipitation	0.00 in	0.10 in	1.43 (1983)
Sea Level Pressure	29.95 in		
Wind Speed	2 mph (North)		
Max Wind Speed	9 mph		
Max Gust Speed	12 mph		
Visibility	6 miles		
Events	Fog		

The Dr. Charles Lectures – Our Place in Time

POL4350 – Political Absolutes Lecture 4

Professor Bailey Charles

Dr. Charles: (in song with soft shoe dance) I stand before you as a liar. Not a king, not a priest, not a squire. Everything I say, should just be thrown away. Because I am nothing but a big fat liar. (End of song). Now let's get started.

Before "now" is a long list of "was's," and there is a seemingly infinite supply of "gonna be's" that will follow "now."

Imagining a single "was" or a single "gonna be" in relation to the total population of each takes on the frame of reference one adopts when considering a single cell in the human body or a single grain of sand on a beach, a single water molecule in the ocean, or a single hydrogen atom in the universe. Mathematically, the relationship is one divided by infinity, which is essentially zero. But that is one "was" divided by the total number of "was's" by everybody and everything.

What about "now"? What about all of the things that are happing right now? All of the "is's." There is an infinite number of "is's" right now. The list that you are making right now is probably a bunch of "was's" and "gonna be's" and very few "is's." How many of the "is's" can you competently keep track of?

What makes you or I think we are somehow important, or that one event is really more important than any other event? Or, put another way, "Why would you or I allow a single "is" which became a "was" to define our life or be the determining influence on the rest of the "gonna be's"?" Are these the right questions to consider?

To go any further, we have to spend a few moments thinking about Einstein's Theory of Relativity: E = mc2, which communicates that all Energy is related to all Matter and that the amount of energy in a piece of matter is proportional to the amount of matter being considered. The thing about energy is that its power per unit area is diluted as the distance from the source is increased. The rate of dilution is $1/r^n$ where "r" is the radius distance from the source and "n" is a decay constant. An "n" equal to 2 will model the dilution of energy in the perfect vacuum of space. A value of "n" greater than 2 is an effort to model energy dilution of limited spectral consideration within a cluttered environment absent a perfect vacuum.

The idea of spectral consideration responds to the notion of Energy being comprised of many emissions that oscillate at specific frequencies. For instance, the energy emitted by a red light bulb is comprised of frequencies that are within the visible spectrum that is red. The light bulb does not emit energies that are readily detected within the range of frequencies associated with the FM radio band or cellular radio band, or blue light, green light, yellow light, and many other frequency bands. My current thinking is that to some degree, all things emit energy along all frequencies but to varying degrees and that not being able to measure something does not confirm its absence.

There is something about oscillations that you need to know before we can go much further, and that is that if there are two or more sources, the net effect of their interactions will be the algebraic sum of the amplitude for a given "now" or span of "now's." If the amplitude of the oscillation from one source at a given time and distance is at its maximum and the amplitude of the oscillation from the second source is at its minimum at the exact same time and place, the net result will be zero if the amplitudes were the same.

So imagine this "now" that you are having. The colors you see are the result of the optical response to the light sources (reflections are treated as secondary sources). The sounds you hear are results of the auditory response to the perturbations of the air medium impacting your eardrum within the oscillating range of human hearing (20 Hz to 20 KHz). The thoughts you are now thinking are the net effect of electro-chemical responses within the neural network of your brain which is influenced by everything in your presence now, every thought you have ever had, and everything that has ever happened to you. These thoughts compel both physiological and psychological conditions that are often referred to as feelings. If the extent to which feelings are dominant exceeds some threshold established by the prevailing wisdom of who are the judges, feelings become obsessions, which become neuroses, which become disorders, and so on. In English, happiness in its most unimaginable extreme will get you to the exact same destinations as sadness, anger, desire, etc.

So all stuff emits energy that is comprised of multiple frequencies and that the nature of the energy signature can impact how we feel. When given the understanding and the option, we can choose what energy sources we expose ourselves to and the nature of that exposure (naked at the source or at some distance with an attenuating medium between us).

It seems to me that seeking out energy sources that help me feel good or nurture my inner purpose makes more sense than seeking out energy sources that make me feel bad or leave me feeling unfulfilled. However, the thing that compelled good at one time in life will not always compel good, and does not compel good in all areas and to all people. So what makes me feel good is time variant, the extent to which people compel good is time variant, and the nature of goodness compelled by a single person is not uniform over the span of "Goodness."

Virtually none of the people that were near me when I was born are near me now. Virtually all of the people near me now are relatively new in my life or can be traced back to after I left the space program. Those people that are no longer near me have either moved on without consideration of its impact on me, as a direct result of considering its impact on me, or as part of their intended path that had nothing to do with me at all. Regardless of why, all I am left with are memories of them. Of the people that are in my life now, their proximity to me is time variant and there are attenuators and filters that I have employed that limit the extent and nature of their impact on me. However, neither the attenuators nor filters are perfect so their impact on me is both inside and outside the realm that I had targeted for impact.

My "now" is the net impact of all the energy that is coming at me and the energy that I am generating. So is yours. I have some control over my passive relationship with the energy sources around me, including people, and I believe I can understand the techniques to optimize the spectral profile of the energy I am emitting and the attenuators and filters I apply. Keeping in mind that the nature of "now" is time-variant, the specific configuration of spectral profile, attenuators, and filters must also be time-variant in order to continue being effective.

It is true that your "now" is the net effect of everything that has ever happened and everyone who has ever lived. However, the effect of all the "was's" on you is dependent on the distance in time and space relative to the source and your spectral, attenuator, and filter profile. Stuff you have never heard of probably has no impact. However, a person who is close to you and is affected by stuff you have never heard of will have impact on you. Once something has impacted you, you will have some memory of it. Over time, that memory will be influenced by all the other stuff that has impacted your life.

Our memories are not recorded facts and they are absolutely not to be considered truths. This is not to say that all memories are all wrong, it is to say that not all memories are all right and when left to our memories, we have no idea which ones are right and which ones are wrong.

Why would a person choose to use a memory as a defining moment in their life and then store it as a shitty event?

English clergyman John Newton (1725–1807), the person given credit for the hymn "Amazing Grace," had one perception of "now" before he wrote the song, a different perception of "now" after he wrote the song, and a different perception towards the end of his life. Over the course of his life, he made the transition from being defined by circumstances to defining circumstances concerning the fundamental question of slavery. Newton's story is the clearest illustration of the notion that people can become aware of flawed thinking and seek a higher truth at the expense of their current value system. There were those who agreed with Newton but their lack of commitment in the moment became a regret on their deathbeds.

Over two hundred years has passed between Newton's death and the time of this lecture but everyone alive today is having an experience that was influenced by the nature of the energy that John Newton chose to emit. All he was doing was influencing a better "now" as he was experiencing it.

The relevance of all this to my life is that my "now" is at an ebbing point in terms of being defined or defining, and I am bored. But worse than being bored, it is the first time in my life that I might have to seek out my next "success at all cost" endeavor and I want to make sure I make the right choices.

I know of so many people that allow the past to define them all the way to their grave. I know a few people that used the past as a foundation to the building of an inspired future. Over the course of my life to this point, I have extensive experience being in the first group and some experience in the second group. Right now, I lack a vision to be in the second group and I would rather die than be in the first group (Please tell me that you see the paradox in a person who would rather die than be defined by circumstances until they died.).

Over the years I have learned to listen for things. Sometimes it is nothing more than paying attention to the bass line in a recorded piece of music and ignoring the rest of the ensemble. Other times it is for the subtle phrases and changes in tone that indicates whether a person is being completely honest or forthcoming. I don't enjoy doing it because it is exhausting. I would rather have all the musicians on separate audio tracks so I could just mute everybody I am not interested in right now and I would certainly prefer to believe that people are telling me the truth and being forthcoming.

In the first case, all of the music I listen to is recorded in stereo so the best I can do is turn down either the left or right channel. In the second case, there is no person who has ever been a recognized part of my life that demonstrated a zealot's commitment for candor in all situations. Even those closest to me have grayed the line of truth, if for no other reason than to surprise me on my birthday. And in the spirit of full disclosure, I do it too. There is no single word that expresses the sentiment to account for all departures from the nucleus of truth. To call them all lies is too general because sometimes a message has nothing to do with the actual words or actions. How often do we tell the people we love that we love them without saying any immediate derivative of the phrase "I love you."?

Think of Truth as a light source of infinite size and brightness. If you are able to do that, you are better than I am because my thought process has concluded that an infinite thing is impossible because it conflicts with the reality of other things. So instead of trying to think of one single powerful thing, let's think of a bunch of smaller things … all of the things that are true. In my mind, the image is that of the night sky and the truths are the stars.

When the sky is clear and the moon is new, the naked eye can see stars and planets that are not visible at other times. Like all of the things that are true, the planets and stars are there whether we see them or not; almost everything we first thought about the stuff in the sky turned out to be wrong or incomplete; our current understanding is still incomplete and biased by our measurement tools and the algorithms we use to analyze the data.

We could all freak out because we don't really know anything or take a more moderate viewpoint that includes the opportunity to experience Truth in all its glory if we clear away the "clouds of bias" and the "moon of false beliefs." I am really sorry about those hokey phrases but I just couldn't help myself. The point is that truth, be it the correct answer to an algebra problem, the best way to treat each other, or anything, will reveal itself to the extent that were are open to it until we are so close its energy burns through our filters and attenuators and, like Icarus who flew too close to the sun, melts our wings and we crash back to Earth.

This idea of getting "too close to the fire" goes back thousands of years and has been written about in numerous ways by people who insisted that they knew what was best for me and that it is dangerous to seek out truth and wisdom on my own. As a successful business person and technical professional who has studied history and those people in the history books, including the history books that are the foundation of many of the religions practicing today, I can comfortably say that I am here for a reason and purpose that is beyond the understanding of any person, alive or dead. But it doesn't make them wrong. It just means that their message is biased by their arrogance and fear.

I don't believe God wants me to be afraid of anything and that God's imminence diminishes any concern as to being offended by something I might say or do. I do believe that naked honesty in thought that is transmitted through a filter whose foundation is love will manifest true greatness.

When I have told the hardest truths, my soul is cleansed.

When I have channeled all my energy towards a goal that brings others joy, my sense of purpose is strengthened.

When I move about the world in which I live taking care to see it all with honest eyes, free of fear or judgment, I tend to look for the quickest route home where I can have an experience free from the Zen-crashing antics of the general public.

The unfortunate things are that I am too young to never leave my home again, so practicality is an issue, and I suspect that my true purpose will manifest itself somewhere other than my home.

But, if I pick my targets carefully, I can still be pretty close to a state of nirvana. But again, I would still like to be in a state of nirvana no matter what.

As in all things, the “no matter what” is what makes life worth living. But be careful how often you use that phrase and what you are talking about when you use it. So no matter what you might think, everything I have said here is a lie and I hope it helps you find the truth.

Thank you.

End of Lecture

Election Day minus 67 days

Weather Report Fujiwhara Beach, FL

Actual	Avg.	Record	
Mean Temperature	82 °F		
Max Temperature	87 °F	85 °F	93 °F (1999)
Min Temperature	77 °F	75 °F	48 °F (2004)
Dew Point	71 °F		
Average Humidity	68		
Maximum Humidity	80		
Minimum Humidity	61		
Precipitation	0.00 in		
Sea Level Pressure	30.02 in		
Wind Speed	7 mph (SE)		
Max Wind Speed	12 mph		
Max Gust Speed	-		
Visibility	10 miles		
Events	None		

Pontification of the MickBill - Energy Independence

Cue Music.

Announcer And now, Pontification of the MickBill.

In the America I now live in, there is an infinite mental capability to solve any technical problem that presents itself or is dreamed of. In the America I dream of, that infinite mental capability would be put to good use and we would redesign our infrastructure so that we would never be reliant on any other nation ever again for those things we need.

Crude oil is a finite resource that produces byproducts that are harmful to living creatures. In addition to it making no sense to rely on it as the fuel for all automobiles, ships, and aircraft, it makes no sense to need to import it in order to meet our demand. The argument to the contrary is shortsighted at best and intellectually dishonest to the point of being criminal at worst. In the America I dream of, we would no longer use petroleum based internal combustion engines except where absolutely necessary and none of the fuel supply would be imported.

Coal, like crude oil, is also a finite resource that produces byproducts that are harmful to living creatures. Unlike crude oil, we have plenty of it and don't need to import it. However, almost half of the electricity produced in the United States is from the burning of coal and we do export it. Playing the tape forward, so to speak, clearly shows an atmosphere containing noxious gasses that we put there and an inability to generate the necessary electricity because the coal is all gone. In the America I dream of, the mining and use of coal will be reduced to the absolute minimum necessary.

Nuclear power, for all its promise is also based on the use of a finite resource and, though it doesn't contribute to the inventory of greenhouse gasses, has its own dangers that have consequences that affect generations of people. I cannot advocate the proliferation of nuclear power plants in order to meet our energy needs because the waste products are so toxic and a minor incident can become a major catastrophe in a matter of moments.

So what do we do? Well, as long as the sun is shining there is opportunity. As long as the wind is blowing there is opportunity. As long as the moon continues to revolve about our planet, there is opportunity. As long as there is water on our planet there is opportunity. And that is just the stuff we do know about. In the America I dream of, we would take advantage of the sunshine, the breeze, the tides, and the molecular composition of water.

The argument against doing such things is based on the current economics resisting the business of "renewable energy." And that is a plausible argument as long as we appeal to our lesser values. In the America I dream of, we would support those who endeavor to build solar panels, windmills, wave generators, and hydrogen production. We would not ask government to get involved because government lacks the innovative thinking to manage the transition. As individuals, we would participate in solving the problem. We would study physics, mathematics, and materials sciences because we realize that we should know more about our planet. We would encourage and help our children in those subjects and support our schools in the teaching of those subjects. In the America I dream of, we would realize that energy independence is our problem and we would do what was necessary to solve it.

There are many ways to make energy independence a reality and there are many books already published on the subject. I encourage everyone to read as many of those books as possible until all of the questions are answered. Then I encourage everyone to ask more questions and look inward to understand what we can do to help us move toward that goal. In the America I dream of, we are all doing everything we can to make the world a better place. Telling other people to change their lives won't get it done, but asking people if they honestly believe they are doing everything they can just might inspire an idea or two.

Cue Music.

Announcer	This has been a Pontification of the MickBill.
Producer	And we're out.

Election Day minus 66 days

Weather Report Fujiwhara Beach, FL

Actual	Avg.	Record	
Mean Temperature	83 °F		
Max Temperature	89 °F	85 °F	95 °F (2005)
Min Temperature	78 °F	75 °F	71 °F (1997)
Dew Point	72 °F		
Average Humidity	69		
Maximum Humidity	80		
Minimum Humidity	61		
Precipitation	0.00 in		
Sea Level Pressure	29.97 in		
Wind Speed	7 mph (SSW)		
Max Wind Speed	15 mph		
Max Gust Speed	-		
Visibility	10 miles		
Events	None		

That Saturday Morning

TGTDTT — Are we getting enough fiber in our diet?

MickBill — I assume you are referring to my pontification. Well I have no explanation for something that has no explanation. It just came out and I am okay with that.

TGTDTT — Any fallout?

MickBill — Well let me bend your ear with my song of life. Someday I will sing it right. These things I feel deep inside my heart are beginning to well up from within. At first I thought it was some demonic possession but the CAT scan didn't show anything. Then I remembered something Professor Charles was talking about in his last lecture.

TGTDTT — What was it?

MickBill — I can't remember exactly what he said, but the intent of what he said helped me understand and empathize with the first settlers. The last thing that any of them needed was people taking their hard earned wages to pay for people to live in squalor and not work. There is no dignity in taking a government subsidy check and it is the epitome of arrogance to believe that a person has the right to seize assets through individual effort and then transfer a portion of those seized assets to people who do no work. It is an affront to everything I understand and believe about God that government seizes assets to sustain its hold in power. Those who look to government for the solutions are looking away from God. I am not saying that people who need help should not be helped, I am saying government sees it as a market sector ripe with growth opportunities. Helping my brother is my responsibility and I can't subcontract that out.

TGTDTT

Now you get it. Now you have to control it. If you run around telling people that you have to tell them what you know then people will perceive you as someone who is not in control of their own thinking. If you run around telling people what they need to do, then you become part of the noise. If you believe people will accept what you are saying to them as the truth then you risk assuming all that comes with the flawed belief that your thinking is truthful. If that happens, then all you are left with is your claim that you are right and nobody listens to that guy.

MickBill

I still have almost a month until the Republican primary and I am rethinking my entire approach to the guests I have scheduled as well as the topics I want to cover.

TGTDTT

The more you plan, the more you have to report to management, the more management has to report to the Federal Communications Commission Office of Information Protocols. If they have already approved your plan, then there is no need to change it.

MickBill — You don't get it. I can't ever do another "What made you want to run for office?" interview ever again. I don't even think I can hide my newfound contempt for many of the candidates. There is no way I can stick to the plan they currently know about.

TGTDTT — No one is asking you to stick to a plan. I am suggesting that you consider keeping the plan and then doing each show within the moment. See each guest as you have never seen them before and then speak to that person.

MickBill — I pride myself on preparing for the interviews I have with my guests and you are asking me to stop doing one of the few things I take pride in doing. What are you going to suggest next? I should stop looking up words in the dictionary to make sure I am using them correctly?

OBandSD — You are resisting and for what? Your pride? Do you have any awards for "interview prep" that you can show us? I have come to notice that every week you order bacon and a biscuit and I am beginning to understand why. The smoky flavor of the bacon drowns out the bitter taste of thinking your pride is on the line. The dry biscuit soaks up the extra stomach acid produced due to the stress of discovering some of what you believe is different from some of the things you think you should believe. I get it. But your pride is tied up in doing your job correctly. What about experiencing life correctly?

MickBill — Well look who finally woke up. At the core of all the reasons for the things I used to be was the firmly held belief that I was and still am fair and honest in every facet of my life. I think it would be wrong to ambush a guest who has accepted an invitation to be on my show.

OBandSD — An ambush requires a plan. A plan has to be approved by management. No one at this table has suggested doing either of those things. We are suggesting that you set aside what you think the audience wants to hear and replace it with what you are really interested in understanding about the person you are interviewing. You say you do that now, but you really don't and you have your cheat sheet right in front of you to keep the conversation going.

MickBill — For a guy who says he doesn't listen to my show, you sure sound like you know a lot about it.

OBandSD — I don't listen to your show. I was just guessing. Looks like I guessed pretty well.

MickBill — Shut up.

OBandSD — Is it true that you are compulsively driven to get in the last word in every conversation?

MikeBill	That is absolutely not true. It might seem that way. Besides, always replying to people is a good way of letting them know you are paying attention.
OBandSD	So it is not true?
MickBill	It is not true.
OBandSD	Really?
MickBill	Really.
OBandSD	Huh. Who would have thought?
MickBill	Well at least one person that I know of.
OBandSD	I am amazed.
MickBill	I am pretty amazing.
OBandSD	I give up.
MickBill	They always do.

Election Day minus 65 days

Weather Report where the Committee meets

Actual	Avg.	Record	
Mean Temperature	83 °F	76 °F	
Max Temperature	92 °F	84 °F	100 °F (1953)
Min Temperature	73 °F	68 °F	49 °F (1934)
Dew Point	69 °F		
Average Humidity	66		
Maximum Humidity	84		
Minimum Humidity	47		
Precipitation	0.00 in	0.09 in	1.98 (1940)
Sea Level Pressure	29.86 in		
Wind Speed	10 mph (SSW)		
Max Wind Speed	17 mph		
Max Gust Speed	23 mph		
Visibility	10 miles		
Events	None		

Homeland Security Summary to Committee

- Population deemed subversive to government remains within current guidelines if a Phase 1 lockdown were required.
- Eighty five out of one hundred voters align themselves with the current two party electoral system.
- The nationalization of industries abroad have exposed weaknesses in the control of sensitive information transmitted over the air or through a network.
- Threats of force to government are numerous. The extent of the threats is unknown.
- The single biggest threat to government is the upcoming nationwide election. It is possible, but not likely that independent candidates could replace party affiliated candidates in many critical offices.

Committee Meeting

We are seeing clear signs.

Three	The pollsters are reporting a sixty eight percent drop in the rate of the response for the various polls.
Five	Voter registrations remain at about the same level overall as two years ago, but the percentage of registered Independents is up. Two years ago, only one in ten voters were registered independents. Today it is one in seven.
One	Both the Republican and Democratic National Committees are reporting a sharp decline in individual contributions. To cover costs, both groups had to lean on their respective revenue streams. Wall Street is the principal source of revenue to the Republicans and the unions are bankrolling the Democrats.
Two	The unions are reporting declines in membership rolls and a general reduction in vertical sales of insurance and sponsored credit cards.
Four	The Chairman of the Federal Reserve is beginning to leave bread crumbs for us to know that the money supply needs to shrink to prevent devaluation of the currency.

One	Professor Charles' most recent lecture captured almost seven million views in the first twenty four hours after it was posted. His lectures tend to draw about thirteen million views before his next lecture is uploaded.
Two	When do we think the good professor is going to visit his brother in Maine again?

Election Day minus 62 days

Weather Report Northfield, VT

Actual	Avg.	Record	
Mean Temperature	65 °F	62 °F	
Max Temperature	73 °F	74 °F	89 °F (1953)
Min Temperature	57 °F	50 °F	36 °F (1970)
Dew Point	59 °F		
Average Humidity	79		
Maximum Humidity	100		
Minimum Humidity	57		
Precipitation	0.04 in	0.09 in	0.83 (1992)
Sea Level Pressure	29.79 in		
Wind Speed	3 mph (SSW)		
Max Wind Speed	14 mph		
Max Gust Speed	22 mph		
Visibility	5 miles		
Events	Fog, Rain		

The Dr. Charles Lectures - Polishing My KarMa

POL4350 – Political Absolutes Lecture 5

Professor Bailey Charles

Dr. Charles

I lie because I choose the words I choose to get you to believe what I want you to believe. It is imperative you hear everything I say through that filter. It is the entertainment this college sells and your parents paid for. Now let us get to business.

For every action, there is an equal and opposite reaction. This is karma. Often we refer to Newton's second law when referring to the set of physical objects that do not include ourselves. What the Eastern mystics understood well before Isaac Newton was a gleam in his father's eye was that energy is the essence of action and the physical bodies that result from aggregation of matter. Therefore, karma, is a five letter word that gives voice to what we happens when we are cowards, liars, thieves, as well as teachers, craftsman, and seekers of truth. And every possible permutation in between and beyond.

Take a moment and allow yourself the opportunity to take inventory of everything you are thinking and feeling at this moment. The inventory you just took and the recollection of the thoughts you had, as well as the original stimuli that produced the thought to begin with are sequential responses to an initial stimuli, or action.

Knowing this might explain why many of you in this class will inherent the family fortune and businesses. It might explain why some of you will enter into politics as either a Democrat or Republican. It might also explain why there are many religions being represented here by all of you.

Knowing this can also be a lifeline back to the energy space in which you existed before your thoughts set off a chain of events that yielded an inventory that include unwanted items.

Knowing this can also be used as a calculus to create a desired inventory of thoughts and feelings.

At our core is the exact same energy source that created the universe. But we all showed up at different times, in different places, and from different parents. Karma then, karma there, and karma their, is the karma that began our karmic "shape" if you will. Shaping continued throughout or lives and continues as we continue.

Imagine for a moment the "shape" of the pure source and now envelope it in the imagined "shape" of your karma.

What you see in your mind's eye right now is why the world is the way it is right now. There is nothing anyone else can do to change what you see in your mind's eye. There is nothing you can do to change what anyone else sees in their mind's eye. The only thing you can do is to appreciate how much you get in the way of allowing God's love to be manifested right here, right now.

Now go listen to a politician.

Thank you.

End of Lecture

Fujiwhara Beach City Council Meeting

Pursuant to Public Notice, Mayor FicChaTwentySeven convened a regular meeting of the City Council in the Council Chamber. Those present were

Mayor FicChaTwentySeven,

Vice-Mayor FicChaTwentySix,

Councilwoman FicChaThirty,

Councilwoman FicChaTwenty,

Councilman FicChaTwoA,

City Attorney FicChaTwentyThree,

And City Manager FicChaTwoBee.

The mayor led a moment of silence and the Pledge of Allegiance.

FicChaTwentySeven	The first order of business is the contract for Healthcare Consulting Services.
FicChaTwoA	I know the woman that started that company.
FicChaTwoB	I met her in college. We both pledged the same sorority.
FicChaTwenty	I make a motion that we approve the contract in its current form.
FicChaThirty	Excuse me. Don't you think we should talk about an open ended commitment for this consultant?
FicChaTwentySix	I second the motion.

FicChaTwentySeven	A motion has been made and seconded. I call for a vote. I vote "Aye"
FicChaTwentySix	"Aye"
FicChaTwenty	"Aye"
FicChaTwoA	"Aye"
FicChaThirty	"Nay"
FicChaTwentySeven	The "Ayes" have it. The motion carries. The next item on the agenda is the improvements to the storm water system in order to meet Florida Department of Environmental Protection requirements.
FicChaTwenty	I make a motion that we approve the contract for engineering and project management services as submitted.
FicChaThirty	This is new and is not mentioned in the budget this council just approved ... how can we discuss it logically?
FicChaTwentySix	I second the motion.
FicChaTwentySeven	A motion has been made and seconded. I call for a vote. I vote "Aye"
FicChaTwentySix	"Aye"
FicChaTwenty	"Aye"
FicChaTwoA	"Aye"
FicChaThirty	"Nay"

FicChaTwentySeven	The "Ayes" have it. The motion carries. The next item on the agenda is the new fee schedule to be adopted by the recreation department.
FicChaTwenty	I make a motion that we approve the fee schedule.
FicChaThirty	The fee change is an across the board increase of ten percent. The revenues forecasted do not account for possible pricing point fall out and are still not sufficient to address the tax payer subsidy of recreation in our city. Can we discuss this in more detail to work out a common sense approach so we don't continue to waste tax payer money?
FicChaTwentySix	I second the motion.
FicChaTwentySeven	A motion has been made and seconded. I call for a vote. I vote "Aye"
FicChaTwentySix	"Aye"
FicChaTwenty	"Aye"
FicChaTwoA	"Aye"
FicChaThirty	"Nay"
FicChaTwentySeven	The "Ayes" have it. The motion carries. That was the last item on the agenda. This meeting is adjourned.
FicChaThirty	I have something to say ...
FicChaTwentySeven	This meeting is adjourned.

Election Day minus 60 days

Weather Report Fujiwhara Beach, FL

Actual	Avg.	Record	
Mean Temperature	84 °F		
Max Temperature	88 °F	84 °F	94 °F (2011)
Min Temperature	79 °F	75 °F	74 °F (2010)
Dew Point	76 °F		
Average Humidity	77		
Maximum Humidity	87		
Minimum Humidity	68		
Precipitation	0.00 in		
Sea Level Pressure	30.08 in		
Wind Speed	7 mph (NE)		
Max Wind Speed	9 mph		
Max Gust Speed	-		
Visibility	10 miles		
Events	None		

Pontification of the MickBill - Immigration

Cue Music.

Announcer — And now, this week's edition of Pontification of the MickBill.

We forget, refused to believe, or were never taught that our ancestors from Europe, Asia, and elsewhere were not the first people to live in the areas we now define as the United States of America. It is also worth noting that the Louisiana Purchase was money paid to the government of France and not paid to those who were living in that region at the time. In short, illegal immigrants of some form founded this country. It was only because our ancestors had better weapons and organization that our borders are what they are and property rights are defined as they are. But it is what it is and we should make the best out of it.

There is value in securing our borders as a means of controlling trade and the proliferation of harmful substances and potential terrorists, but deportation doesn't seem to accomplish anything but a strain on the taxpayer. If we catch someone trying to enter the country without observing the process and protocols, turning them around makes no sense. Deporting someone who has been arrested for committing a crime because they are not in this country legally makes no sense. So if we catch them at the border, fine. If they are smart enough to get in the country and are productive members of society and do not commit any crimes, so be it.

All of the other arguments regarding illegal immigration diminish in their validity.

Besides, what right does a government have to criminalize working hard in order to feed your family? The argument that everybody who enters into this country is committing a crime and that there is no statute of limitations indicts not only our founding fathers, but also every single person whose ancestors immigrated to this country. There is no way to see it any other way and still maintain even a modicum of intellectual honesty. The bottom line is that today we have an attitude towards illegal immigration that is hypocritical. In the America of my dreams, our policy of limiting access through the border crossings and patrolling the borders as we currently do would continue. However, we would not actively hunt down people who made it into the country and prevent them from engaging in beneficial activities in order to support themselves and their families. What we would do is prosecute all of the crimes typically associated with illegal immigrants in the manner to be proposed and would condition all access to the services offered to citizens on being able to prove citizenship.

The bottom line is that every reasonable effort to prevent illegal immigration would be continued, anyone found guilty of committing an illegal act in the country would be dealt with quickly and permanently, and only citizens would enjoy the benefits of citizenship. As draconian as this may seem, these actions would clearly delineate citizens from non-citizens and permanently deal with individuals who demonstrate an inability to be productive and beneficial elements of the America of my dreams. Individuals who assist illegal immigrants will be dealt with quickly and permanently. Dealing with matters of immigration in this matter will remove all incentives to come to this country illegally and all incentives to provide material support, including employment, to illegal immigrants.

But if a person manages to get into this country and never commits a crime of any sort, do we care if they are here illegally? They won't be able to get a driver's license, social security card, ID, bank account, employment, or access to any government service, which means they have to pay cash for everything and rely on public transportation or walk.

The downside to my approach is that our strawberries, lawn care, and maid services will become more expensive. But so what.

Cue Music.

Announcer — This has been a Pontification of the MickBill.

Producer — And we're out.

Election Day minus 59 days

Weather Report Fujiwhara Beach, FL

Actual	Avg.	Record	
Mean Temperature	84 °F		
Max Temperature	89 °F	84 °F	92 °F (2011)
Min Temperature	78 °F	75 °F	71 °F (1999)
Dew Point	75 °F		
Average Humidity	77		
Maximum Humidity	85		
Minimum Humidity	62		
Precipitation	0.10 in		
Sea Level Pressure	30.04 in		
Wind Speed	5 mph (East)		
Max Wind Speed	20 mph		
Max Gust Speed	-		
Visibility	10 miles		
Events	Rain, Thunderstorm		

That Saturday Morning

TGTDTT comes from a place and grew up in a time that forced him to ask really hard questions about the world in which he lived and the role he was to play. It has taken almost a half century of searching so far and he is not done yet, but there are some ideas that seemed to be bearing fruit.

The first idea is that every single thing, living or not, human or not, comes from the same source and that non-humans are less exceptional than humans with regards to the rules governing their behavior. Now when I use the phrase "less exceptional," I am making reference to the number of exceptions or contradictions to the rules that govern or explain their behavior. They are not less interesting.

Those non-human creations from the same source that created humans observe a code of conduct that may be described with mathematical precision and a quantified confidence factor – and there are no exceptions. There are computational uncertainties that may be construed as error, but the extent of the error is quantified. For all of the "anomalous" behavior that humans are capable of, TGTDTT believes that every single person will devote their entire life, heart and soul, to manifesting their world view on this earth. The reason TGTDTT believes this is because that is what people do. Even a person who only complains is devoted to manifesting the reality that he or she really has something to say. The reason things are the way they are is because that is what we are all working together to create.

MickBill would not be joining TGTDTT this Saturday morning. It wasn't the first time one or both of them had someplace they had to be. It was the first time TGTDTT decided to go to breakfast without him.

The regular table, the regular waitress brought coffee on her first stop, the meal on the second stop, and the bill on the third stop.

Maybe MickBill being absent was a good thing for the time being because it would be the first time TGTDTT would be introducing his new found acquaintance to the joys of his daily life. For some reason, the waitress knew not to bring TGTDTT's guest anything. She did not even speak to him when she came by. TGTDTT just assumed it was supposed to be that way. It seemed as though whenever he was hanging out with FicChaZero, everything went extremely smooth.

TGTDTT	This worked out well.
FicChaZero	Do you not appreciate the humor in your deciding that the current state of affairs is dependent on your articulated opinion?
TGTDTT	Is there a way to know when saying how you feel might lessen the essence of the feeling itself.
FicChaZero	Do you not believe that the greatest of truths are concealed by the greatest web of lies?
TGTDTT	Well there is no point in telling you about how much I enjoyed my breakfast.

Election Day minus 58 days

Weather Report where the Committee meets

Actual	Avg.	Record	
Mean Temperature	71 °F	74 °F	
Max Temperature	82 °F	83 °F	104 °F (1881)
Min Temperature	60 °F	66 °F	46 °F (1924)
Dew Point	57 °F		
Average Humidity	62		
Maximum Humidity	78		
Minimum Humidity	45		
Precipitation	0.00 in	0.11 in	3.78 (1934)
Sea Level Pressure	30.06 in		
Wind Speed	7 mph (South)		
Max Wind Speed	16 mph		
Max Gust Speed	18 mph		
Visibility	10 miles		
Events	None		

Homeland Security Summary to Committee

- Population deemed subversive to government remain within current guidelines if a Phase 1 lockdown were required.

- Eighty four out of one hundred voters align themselves with the current two party electoral system.

- The nationalization of industries abroad have exposed weaknesses in the control of sensitive information transmitted over the air or through a network.

- Threats of force to government are numerous. The extent of the threats is unknown.

- The single biggest threat to government is the upcoming nationwide election. It is possible, but not likely that independent candidates could replace party affiliated candidates in many critical offices.

Committee Meeting

Dr. Charles knows.

One	I had a dream last night in which I saw the world through the eyes of all the people who sat in the chair in which I now park my posterior. I awoke this morning knowing this could all go away if we do not heed the warnings.
Two	Please tell me that you all see what is happening. All of the analysis shows that at the source of this shift are these videos.
Three	Nice try. All of the analysis shows that at the source of this shift are the lectures given by Dr. Charles.
Four	The good professor knows of his mention in this room. He knows who we are and what that means. He knows that if he is not careful, we will create monuments in his name and then destroy his reputation while he is alive, then kill him when nobody cares any longer. One thing is certain, he knows we are going to kill him one day.
Five	I don't like it when they know about us.
Two	There is a Judas in this room.
Four	How could the professor not know we exist? He grows up in Maine. After completing his undergraduate engineering studies at MIT, he accepts a position in

the Classified Missions Office at NASA. His role was to assume his post at the Launch Console if a Phase 1 Lockdown were ordered. The background investigation showed a person of incredible integrity and his word could be trusted. While at Kennedy Space Center he earned a Master's and Doctorate in Physics. When the Space Shuttle Program ended, all of Dr. Charles' knowledge set and training became obsolete. In fact, his relevance to us went away when the Department of Defense, the National Security Agency, and the Central Intelligence Agency withdrew all commitments to use the space shuttle for their needs. Dr. Charles drifted a bit when an old friend from elementary school came across his resume while searching for Ph.D.'s who might want to teach at a small college in Vermont. What I am just telling you now is that the investigation also revealed an almost eidetic memory and the compulsive need to connect information.

Two

Take a guy who might benefit from some form of medication, train him to be a critical element in the support of government in a time of crisis, and then have him spend out his days in the quiet solitude of a rural New England college for the spoiled, to give lectures on anything he wants to talk about and the students will receive college credit towards a Bachelor's of Arts in Human Studies. Someone gave this guy too much free time. Has he told anybody?

Four There are no indications that he has. My read is that he doesn't care. If he dies, he dies. He would rather not because of his responsibilities as being the highest functioning member in his immediate family, but there is nothing he can do about it. What he won't do is change his position on any issue, look for a fight, entertain the possibility of a fight, or fight. He absolutely doesn't see a fight. He sees a reality, breaks it down in his analytical mind, and tells a group of privileged students what he has come up with. The college seems to think his lectures are valuable. The students seem to think so as well. The good doctor immediately recognized a reality that was the only plausible explanation for the role he played at NASA. There was a plan in place to command certain citizens to be at their post in the event that all other people were ordered off the streets and into their homes. There was no way he did not know that a small group of people decided whether he needed to report to work on any given day.

Two But why hasn't he said anything.

Four There is gene that runs through his family lineage that would indicate to someone that any idea or statement of belief he would make could be attributed to one of the psychological disorders that run through his family. He learned a long time ago to keep the weird stuff to himself. He wouldn't be the first person we had

	diagnosed with schizophrenia and carted off and he knows that. Besides, he really has no interest in selling any of his ideas to anybody. His agenda in class is seemingly harmless and stress free. The reason he is where he is doing what he is doing has absolutely nothing to do with us.
Two	How do we get people to just forget he ever existed? How do we get them to forget what he ever said?
Five	You are suggesting a …
Two	I know what I am suggesting.
One	It has been tried before and it has always failed. Even if you wipe out a whole generation, we will find ourselves right back at this place.
Three	What about two generations?

Election Day minus 55 days

Weather Report Northfield, VT			
Actual	Avg.	Record	
Mean Temperature	61 °F	60 °F	
Max Temperature	74 °F	71 °F	89 °F (2002)
Min Temperature	47 °F	48 °F	33 °F (1953)
Dew Point	57 °F		
Average Humidity	86		
Maximum Humidity	93		
Minimum Humidity	79		
Precipitation	0.56 in	0.10 in	0.98 (1993)
Sea Level Pressure	30.08 in		
Wind Speed	4 mph (SSE)		
Max Wind Speed	12 mph		
Max Gust Speed	15 mph		
Visibility	8 miles		
Events	Rain		

The Dr. Charles Lectures - Underprivileged

POL4350 – Political Absolutes Lecture 6

Professor Bailey Charles

Cue Music, Cue lights, cut to Camera 1

You Host — Good Evening to all of you here in the audience and to our TV, radio, and internet audiences. Tonight's dream conversation is with a relatively unknown professor of Physics at an obscure college in the back woods of Vermont. In addition to promoting his latest book, "The Riches of Nothingness," Dr. Bailey B. Charles, is here to entertain and possibly enlighten us. Ladies and Gentlemen, please join me in welcoming to the dais, Dr. Bailey B. Charles.

Cue "Applause Light" for studio audience. Three seconds. "Applause Light" to "Off."

Dr. Charles — Thank you for letting me speak here today. And I want to be as up front as I can about letting you know that I will be lying to you throughout the evening in order to get you to believe something I want you to believe. I will even go as far as to lie to you about what I believe in if I think it will help me to get you to believe what I want you to believe.

There are murmurs throughout the theatre audience.

Dr. Charles But with every false phrase I utter, I am desperate to the core with hope that you uncover the truth. All I ask is that you tell everyone that you were able to find the truth because Bailey Charles stood right here on this stage and lied to you. He told me that he was going to lie to me and told me that his lies will help me see the truth. What a great guy, even though he is a confessed liar.

The studio becomes almost silent as the mood of the speaker and the audience become more harmonically aligned. But the show was only an hour long and, even though the live airing was commercial free, Bailey Charles had a pretty good idea of what the editors were going to do with the recordings for other shows. More importantly, Bailey Charles, knew what the Department of Homeland Security was likely to do with the recordings. The Federal Bureau of Investigation already had a file on him going back some thirty years when he received his first security clearance while working on NASA's Space Shuttle Program in the Classified Missions office. Back then, back there, a security clearance was easy to get and easy to keep because there was a general feeling that only real Americans who were born here were safe so as long as you are a native with no prior convictions or outstanding warrants, "Welcome to the world of stuff you are not allowed to talk to other people about. Remember that you took an oath to defend our stuff with your life or we will do unspeakable things to you." Today, things are different.

Today, the security people look for identifiable trends in an observable data set. There are statistics and the people who make their living from government can mine a great deal of data. The question becomes, "What is a reportable data spike?" Which begs the question, "Who does the report go to?" and the answer is that the person who received the most votes for the particular governmental office decides the answers to those questions. If the person elected to be the commander in chief was voted into office on a platform of "You need me to protect you and I will do everything in my power to make sure you are safe." Then the public accepts that lots of data will be mined, but not to worry.

Dr. Bailey Charles is worried because he knows the FBI file with his name on it is much larger than when it started and has been copied more times than one might be comfortable with. Since the publication of his first book, he has been audited by the Internal Revenue Service each year for the previous seven years. The president of the small college at which Dr. Bailey Charles is a tenured professor, has been visited by people who work for important people and told that it would be perfectly acceptable if the fungible nature of Dr. Charles' function at the college were re-examined. The college president was also told that his personal fortunes were tied to the distance between the college and Dr. Bailey Charles. But it had to be done so that everything Bailey Bernard Charles had ever done was devalued or discredited.

Someone somewhere has a concern that people are listening to Bailey Bernard Charles, Ph.D. and it threatens the security of the government of the United States of America and could potentially destabilize the governmental structure of the entire world.

What could he have possibly done or said to make him so dangerous to the power elite? Other than being a college professor who has written a couple of books to keep his publishing quota up, Bailey Bernard Charles leads no political or professional groups, he belongs to no fraternities or secret societies, has never been arrested or questioned, or even sued anyone in civil court. The college at which he teaches services a small and undistinguished student body. The college is accredited, but none of the alumni have ever been elected to high office, run a Fortune 500 company, or been mentioned in People magazine for that matter. Could the concern be due to the idea that the internet audience for Dr. Charles' lectures and speeches is growing and the resulting chatter is causing reporting spikes for key phrases that indicate a potential for a voter mandated shift in operations, as defined and implemented at the National Security Agency.

Bailey Charles was always a smart guy who didn't care what people thought of what he thought. When he knew he was right, he could care less if you believed him. Over the years he has mellowed somewhat, but he still doesn't care what anyone thinks and he doesn't care if you believe him. Now that he has had tenure for a few years, his enjoyment of his time spent in front of a classroom has increased immensely. He came to appreciate that all the facts in the world do not matter to a person who can choose to believe something else. So his lectures became less about facts intended for recitation on an upcoming exam and more of an experience that helped his students tap into a belief system that would never betray them. But the last thing he wanted to do was to become a celebrity of any sort. Over time his classroom attendance had grown to a point that the lectures had to be moved to the lecture auditorium and from there to the college's theatre that can seat the entire student population and faculty. The benefit of using the college theatre was that it was already wired for closed circuit recordings of live events which were then uploaded to the college on line reference library, which included links to YouTube.

It was common for students not to remember anything he said during the lecture. When asked, the students would respond that they clearly understood what the professor was telling them and they will remember the experience for the rest of their lives, but they cannot remember exactly what was said or exactly what the professor was telling them.

Since receiving tenure, the college graduates that listened to Dr. Charles' lectures are registered independent voters, do not contribute to any political party or their candidate, vote in every election, and in every precinct where there is a cluster of Dr. Charles' Alumni, the candidate with no party affiliation does proportionately well. Since the airing of the lecture videos posted in the Internet by students, and now the college, viewership is causing spikes and correlation flags with respect to the decline in membership in any political party and the rise in successful independent candidates. The most alarming thing to Homeland Security is that analysis of the trends using the techniques to forecast hurricanes and game out strategies on how best to survive a global nuclear war is that every one of their jobs were designated for closure. Not some of the jobs, but all of the jobs because the voters are trending towards a government structure that reduces the federal government's role to setting tariffs with foreign nations and collecting import fees. National defense was no longer a major priority. The entire Military Industrial Complex was in jeopardy.

The patterns in the specific text monitored by the National Security Agency and correlated against public records, including voting history and arrest records, and applied to the election results for all elections in the United States during Dr. Charles' humble career show that he is a channel for human advancement which translates into the affected governments being completely overhauled. When the rumors about government taking notice became actions people began taking, Bailey Charles made no mention of it to anyone. When the college president came to him after the visit from some people who work for important people, Dr. Charles had no response to the charges or the threat to be fired. The two men had known each other for many years, were brethren in the service to man and learned men in the history of mankind. There was nothing to be said and it would be the last time it would ever be mentioned again.

Now back to the lecture.

Dr. Charles	Governance is the recognition that some people control other people which is why the first post-revolution act of the winning government is to get other governments to

recognize you. Citizens have to recognize they are citizens in order to recognize a governing element. Government elements recognize other government elements. If a government element does not recognize another government element then resources are expended to either force recognition or get the recognized government back in power.

Privilege is an arbitrary construct that attempts to manifest an unnatural, and therefore artificial, set of social classes. Privilege is the mechanism by which power is quantified. On this earth, a person capable of extending privilege is a powerful person. The greater the privileges that can be extended, the greater the power of the individual extending the privileges.

There are people on this earth that have privileges that other people on this earth do not have. Or so it might seem. If you believe such things, then I know a politician who might like to speak to you.

The phrase "underprivileged" and all its derivations are intended to fester or antagonize the notion that some people are better off than others and it doesn't have to be that way. Of the two times in history of which I am somewhat educated of such a technique being used to incite a government over-throw, the first was in the year 1918 in a Eurasian country called Russia. The second time it was done was in 1957 on a small island in the Caribbean. In both cases, anybody who voiced an idea was either imprisoned or executed. So it seems to me that when someone talks about helping the underprivileged, they are really saying that fewer people will have any privileges if they get into power.

There was a time when a relatively young man ran for the office of the President of the United States, on a platform of "everybody needs to pay their fair share for the services people want." This same person was re-elected four years later using the same campaign speeches from his first campaign. The winning strategy was to make it clear that only a special few were spared the burden of paying for the services government provides and that his plan was stick it to "the rich" to pay for increasing the breadth of services provided by the federal government. The effective majority of voters thought it was a good plan and that this person had the answers. The voters, at least the ones who voted for him, saw this person as their personal savior. By voting for him, they were betting that he would write some words that would take care of them.

During the man's eight years in office, the national debt and the federal budget doubled in size and the Gross Domestic Product of the United States of America stayed about the same. At the state, county, and local levels, the budgets were either reduced or remained the same while the tax base was reduced through unemployment or stagnant property values. But for eight years, the President of the United States of America and his wife took separate and joint vacations to exotic resorts all over the world at the tax payers' expense. Today the former president is making speeches for exorbitant fees and collecting million dollar book deals for books about how other people need to give more to charity and government.

The "underprivileged" have to see themselves as underprivileged before they will ever begin to think that something needs to change. The voice telling others they are underprivileged is the same voice that convinced Eve that she needed to eat from the "Tree of Knowledge." In the end, everybody who thought they were underprivileged are worse off than they were before and the person who got them to believe he had the answers is off making speeches for exorbitant fees and collecting million dollar book deals for books about how other people need to give more to charity and government.

The idea of privilege exists when a person believes that the source from which they came is different from the source from which other people came. This is one of the reasons why family bonds are given importance. The argument is strengthened by a physical and traceable blood line. When the audience needs to be larger than what a family can provide, the bonds of belief systems are given importance, such is the case with religious and political belief systems. The person who believes "best" is at the top of the hierarchy. Those who can either understand the person at the top and convert it to actionable items for the ever increasing masses represent the first level or ring by which privilege may be extended. Each of those individuals is surrounded by a ring of individuals, and so on.

There is, and will always be, a governing hierarchy. Regardless of the form it takes, it has power only when the people give it power. In the United States of America, every even year, there are elections when some people become voters that choose the people that will govern them in this world. The choice a voter makes in the privacy of the voting booth is the single biggest statement the average person will make about their connection to God. Each voter is free to tell anyone anything regarding the choices they made, but no one ever need to know the choice that was actually made. At the core of your vote is the understanding that no one will ever understand your relationship with God so there is no point talking about it and the people you vote for and the issues you approve are the clearest indicators of your faith in God.

The privileges that are extended to each and every one of you are the leftovers that some guy above him did not want. What if we did not let the guy above him have the choice? Absent that, what if we replaced the guy above him with a guy who saw it as an absolute wrong to believe it was his choice to make in the first place.

Good Night

Camera shot goes to wide. The people are standing in applause. Dr. Charles speaks off mic to the Host and leaves the dais stage left. The host approaches the microphone.

Your Host — Thank you everyone for attending this evening's lecture. Good night.

Election Day minus 53 days

Weather Report Fujiwhara Beach, FL		
Actual	Avg.	Record
Mean Temperature	82 °F	
Max Temperature	85 °F	84 °F 90 °F (2010)
Min Temperature	78 °F	75 °F 73 °F (2001)
Dew Point	72 °F	
Average Humidity	74	
Maximum Humidity	82	
Minimum Humidity	65	
Precipitation	0.00 in	
Sea Level Pressure	29.98 in	
Wind Speed	6 mph (ESE)	
Max Wind Speed	10 mph	
Max Gust Speed	-	
Visibility	10 miles	
Events	Thunderstorm	

Pontification of the MickBill - Medical Care

Cue Music.

Announcer — And now, this week's edition of Pontification of the MickBill.

The argument that a longer average lifespan points to an improvement in society at large is countered by all of the problems that result from people living longer and more people living together.

It can be shown that a reduction in infant mortality rates results in increased unemployment and crime. It can also be shown that the increase in the diagnoses of cancer and Alzheimer's is the inevitable result of keeping people alive longer. We all know the grandmother or aunt who spent the last decade of her life dependent on medication to ward off the conditions that were intended to weed her out at a younger age. The horrible decline towards the end where the emphasis is only on keeping the body functioning until there is no heartbeat. In some cases, the heartbeat and respiration is being artificially sustained with machines resulting in an even more inhumane passing.

So what are we really talking about when the subject of medical care comes to mind? It must be completely understood that we are just passing through on our way to someplace else. If that were not true, then we would not care about any of this stuff. So we are talking about doing a whole bunch of something with the knowledge that it will never be finished or solved. An infinite amount of money could be spent and people would still die.

The people selling universal health care are the same people that sell religion and the same people who sell used cars. If there was ever a Faustian type scenario on a large scale, it is the willingness to believe the promises being made about the "Affordable Health Care Act" that is going to be implemented. The essence of the law is that every American taxpayer will fund the medical and pharmaceutical industry at a rate determined by the federal government and Uncle Sam gets his slice of the pie first. The legislation also opens brand new revenue streams for the lawmakers because of lobbying that will now be required because government will be approving all purchases and procedures.

... The congressman from Delaware would be happy to discuss the inclusion of one sentence in the authorization bill that guarantees you are the sole source provider of catheters ...

... The senator from Maine sees no reason not to include the requirement that everyone in the country gets a hernia exam every two years.

From the very beginning, socialized medicine does not work on a large scale because healthcare is an individual choice that cannot be managed by strangers. The only thing it can be is a line item in a budget with calculated projections and statistical performance metrics.

I still believe there is far too much talk about a long life and not enough action living a full life. It has been my experience that being willing to die doing what I believe is right will keep me plenty healthy and happy until my ticket gets punched. I don't start getting sick until that belief begins to fade. I suspect that if more people lived their life like that, the government's charade would have been transparent and we would keep government out of our healthcare. But they don't. Look to Russia, England, Italy, Spain, and Greece for examples of what we can expect.

I love my grandmothers and I love my aunts. My memories

of them are the days when they were vibrant. Each of my grandmothers experienced a decline of such ghastly nature because the medical industry took control of the situation and threw extreme resources towards holding back the one thing that was supposed to take them quickly when they were still living their lives with dignity. In each case, there was a complete transfer of responsibility to the professionals. If a person wants to live and fight these diseases is their choice. There is an institutionalized thinking that a person has to live at all costs which is nothing more than a sales pitch to consume as much of your available resources as possible in the hopeless attempt to postpone the inevitable.

A universal right is something that cannot be stopped unless the person chooses not to exercise it. No one can stop a person from exercising those rights which are universal to all of us. All of the rest of this stuff about healthcare being a universal right is a money grab by the federal government. The words of the Affordable Health Care Act that define the manner in which money is taken from individuals and then applied to the bureaucracy. It further describes the extent to which the government intends to punish any individual who doesn't live up to the terms set forth in the law. It was a hostile acquisition of the health care industry. All of the cost estimates being published are proof beyond proof that there is an equation that predicts how much money every single person involved is going to make because of this new law.

So if Grandma falls and no one knows it until the odor alerts the neighbors, it might be sad, but we are the ones that allowed that to happen. If we pay someone to look in on her so that we can take our vacations, we are deluding ourselves that we are showing how much we love her. If we allow her to involuntarily become one of the bodies that get sucked dry by the medical industry, we are guilty of the worst kind of inhumanity. If Grandma is so important to you, then call her. But if you think that putting her into a home where the care she will receive is better than the care she would receive in your home, you are wrong. Unless Grandma really isn't that important to you.

Cue Music.

Announcer	This has been a Pontification of the MickBill.
Producer	And we're out.

Election Day minus 52 days

Weather Report Fujiwhara Beach, FL

Actual	Avg.	Record	
Mean Temperature	82 °F		
Max Temperature	87 °F	84 °F	91 °F (2005)
Min Temperature	76 °F	75 °F	73 °F (2001)
Dew Point	73 °F		
Average Humidity	77		
Maximum Humidity	89		
Minimum Humidity	57		
Precipitation	0.00 in		
Sea Level Pressure	29.89 in		
Wind Speed	6 mph (South)		
Max Wind Speed	13 mph		
Max Gust Speed	-		
Visibility	10 miles		
Events	Thunderstorm		

That Saturday Morning

Zero nine hundred came early this morning for TGTDTT. He was up late the previous night watching movies he had already seen and probably didn't need to see in the first place. But such is life. But as he was watching, he began thinking about the patterns by which certain movies are replayed. That got him thinking about which TV series get renewed and which don't. And that got him thinking about which cancelled TV shows are in reruns. And that got him thinking about the way Howard Hughes would hold up in his darkened Las Vegas Hotel room watching old westerns on TV. It was with that thought that TGTDTT decided four in the morning was too late to be up watching movies he had already seen.

TGTDTT	Gentlemen. FicChaTen, to what do we owe the honor of your presence?
FicChaTen	MickBill told me you would be here and it had been a while.
MickBill	What about me? You wanted to see me this morning as well.
TGTDTT	There are no candidates for Fujiwhara Beach City Council.
FicChaTen	Everybody has given up. We've asked others with similar slants on small and efficient government to run, but no one wants to go through what we and our families went through trying to help this god-forsaken city gets its fiscal house in order.
TGTDTT	I am just surprised that nobody has thrown their hat in the ring for the two seats.

FicChaTen	What is the point? You will still be just one of five votes and there are three votes that will always vote against you. Plus, the vileness and vehemence of the very vocal Good Old Boy minority is ungodly ... spooky-weird, even for small town politics. As I said when I ran, they must be hiding something ... and they certainly don't want anyone to find it! Either that or their self-worths depend on having some sort of "power" or "control" ... whatever that means in this 2.5 square mile little berg. Or both. Probably both.
TGTDTT	How are things looking for County District 4?
FicChaTen	It is hard to say. It is not like there is any polling to speak of.
MickBill	I think things are looking pretty good for our guy.
TGTDTT	What about State Representative District 53 or Senate District 16.
FicChaTen	Which ones are those?
TGTDTT	District 53 is just a curiosity thing, we can't vote in that district. We will be voting for Senate District 16 though.
FicChaTen	Okay. I am with you now.
TGTDTT	I worked with this guy who remarked during the Casey Anthony trial that he knew she was innocent, the moment he saw her breasts.

MickBill	What is your point?
TGTDTT	Say what you will, but the female Republican challenging the Republican Incumbent is just hot. She is the first political candidate that gets hotter as you get closer to her. I don't know about you guys, but she makes me think thoughts.
FicChaTen	She is pretty sharp too. So don't cut her short. Plus, I get the feeling she has more integrity in her little finger than her long-time Good Old Boy incumbent opponent has in his entire body.
TGTDTT	I'm not cutting her short. I am saying that the closer I got to her at the fund raiser, when she came over and spoke to me, I wanted her to keep talking. But then I had a concern about my saying something that might warrant an apology to her and her husband. Then I thought that the reason I was having these thoughts is because she is right in front of me just talking away. I owe it to her and her family to vote for her as my sincerest form of praise. I trust her to get some good words written in Tallahassee more than I trust myself not to say something extremely inappropriate.
MickBill	You have never worried about saying something inappropriate before.
TGTDTT	This is different. She is the prom queen, class president, student debate champion, and year book editor and she is talking to

me right now as though I matter. I remembered this one time I took my older brother out for his birthday and all he wanted to do was spend some time in a local folk dancing arena. After a few hours I knew it was time to leave because my brother began to believe that one of the dancers actually liked him. Somewhere in my head, I flashed backed to that evening except I was playing the role of my brother and the candidate was playing the role of the dancer. Now I can't look at her without a vivid image as to what I imagine she looks like in a bikini. I married the last woman who made me feel that way and I am still married to her. She gets my vote, but I am keeping my distance.

MickBill — She wants to be taken seriously.

TGTDTT — I do take her seriously.

FicChaTen — Why are you curios about State Representative District 53?

TGTDTT — Republican Primary, two candidates. Candidate A is the incumbent. Candidate B is the challenger. Candidate A is a Mike Haridopolis wanna be. Academically, he is more than his predecessor. Politically he is much less. The challenger is a young guy who did his undergrad at Paris Island and his post-doctoral in the back of a C5 transport taking fire over the deserts of Iraq. I met him a few times and I can't help but see him as a guy that not only deserves respect but wants to lead a group of people in the battle to reverse some of the holds the federal government has gotten on how the state is run. He is physically imposing yet very approachable. If he gets elected, I can see him being a force for change. I don't know anything about the incumbent, but the challenger believes he has a reason to challenge.

FicChaTen I met him. Good people. Semper fi! Speaking of which, you guys know who to thank for keeping the Florida Senate District 16 Republican Primary a closed primary?

TGTDTT I first got it from FicChaSixteen and thought it was one of those things that he says that I don't really need to pay any attention to. I did forward the email to FicChaTwelve so that he would know what is being said about him. He confirmed it. It took me a couple of days to remember that he was a registered Democrat. FicChaThirteen must be concerned.

FicChaTen She found out AFTER he had done it … we were on my boat headed up to the Marina Bar when he told her.

MickBill Wouldn't you have loved to have been a fly on the wall when they got home?

TGTDTT No. I wouldn't.

MickBill Well I would. Entertaining is an understatement.

Election Day minus 51 days

Weather Report where the Committee meets

Actual	Avg.	Record	
Mean Temperature	65 °F	72 °F	
Max Temperature	73 °F	80 °F	94 °F (1980)
Min Temperature	56 °F	63 °F	46 °F (1911)
Dew Point	44 °F		
Average Humidity	51		
Maximum Humidity	66		
Minimum Humidity	35		
Precipitation	0.00 in	0.13 in	4.07 (1966)
Sea Level Pressure	30.07 in		
Wind Speed	10 mph (NNW)		
Max Wind Speed	18 mph		
Max Gust Speed	26 mph		
Visibility	10 miles		
Events	None		

Homeland Security Summary to Committee

- Population deemed subversive to government remain within current guidelines if a Phase 1 lockdown were required.

- Eighty three out of one hundred voters align themselves with the current two party electoral system.

- The nationalization of industries abroad have exposed a weakness in the control of sensitive information transmitted over the air or through a network.

- Threats of force to government are numerous. The extent of the threats is unknown.

- The single biggest threat to government is the upcoming nationwide election. It is possible, but not likely that independent candidates could replace party affiliated candidates in many critical offices.

Committee Meeting

The termination date is set.

Three	We are exposed. We know we are exposed. That means that others also know that we are exposed. But we do not know how large or well known it is currently and if that audience is increasing.
Five	Believe it or not, we have a bigger problem than being taken over by a foreign government.
Three	How can little ole Dr. Charles and his internet videos be a more serious problem than the uncontrolled access to classified information.
Five	Your fear is a government takeover. If that were to happen, that government would have the same problem we do right now. If we solve the Dr. Charles problem, any government who would seek to take us over, would be in our debt. All of the friendly governments would also be in our debt. If we solve the Dr. Charles problem, government takeovers will cease for at least three or four generations.
Four	How long does "squashing the Tucker" really buy us?
One	The fallout from an intervention will be proportional to the momentum of the events at

	that time. The sooner the better. But if we can't do it sooner, then we should do it at a time when there is so much other stuff going on, the story will get buried.
Two	The noisiest news day of the year is Election Day.
Two	How would we communicate our tacit agreement to others?
One	We would tell them that the professor's last lecture seems imminent and that all of his published lectures are national treasures that should only be studied at the highest levels of government.
Three	What do we want to be told?
One	I want to be told that Homeland Security has fixed the leaks in their systems.

Election Day minus 48 days

Weather Report Northfield, VT

Actual	Avg.	Record	
Mean Temperature	46 °F	57 °F	
Max Temperature	60 °F	68 °F	80 °F (1992)
Min Temperature	31 °F	46 °F	29 °F (1948)
Dew Point	36 °F		
Average Humidity	74		
Maximum Humidity	100		
Minimum Humidity	47		
Precipitation	0.00 in	0.11 in	1.24 (1999)
Sea Level Pressure	30.44 in		
Wind Speed	2 mph (West)		
Max Wind Speed	8 mph		
Max Gust Speed	13 mph		
Visibility	7 miles		
Events	Fog		

The Dr. Charles Lectures - The Four Valleys

Mortality is known to all of us, but to Dr. Charles, it is a summons and its messenger had told him of its imminent arrival. Whatever scripts or storylines had been established prior to this moment, Bailey Bernard Charles' connection to "Now" is greater than ever. If you remember a previous lecture, "Now equals the weighted sum of all "Was's" and all "Is's."" and his surrendering to his fate has allowed him to be influenced and guided in ways he never imagined possible. It is almost as if he has become a portal that "Was's" can come through freely with no interpretation. It is as if a "Was" was giving the lecture and not Dr. Charles.

POL4350 – Political Absolutes Lecture 7

Professor Bailey Charles

Dr. Charles

Today I will lie using lies that I was told as a child.

For instance, I was told that the person who was my mother was my aunt and that I had lots of uncles. I was told my value was dependent on the moods and personalities of those around me. I was told Santa Claus was not coming to my house because I was bad. I was also told that I was funny, intelligent, clever, and many other things.

The people who were closest to me in proximity and genetic composition were the sources of the harshest of lies. The contributors to my physical composition were the sources of those lies that will render a person with no justifiable impetus to continue their own existence. In fact, there was no overwhelming data that showed the necessity for a male and female to combine genetic material for another person to enter the world, but I needed a completely different data set to draw from if I were to mitigate the continuation of certain ideas and behaviors.

I could not understand how disagreement became anger and there were many disagreements in my sphere of observability. I began my journey in an environment that the loudest was the most right and getting the credit for being right was everything. All within the belief that included any lack of credit to you was due to the stupidity of everybody else.

As my sphere of observability continued to grow through activities beyond the direct influence of my parents and siblings, my data set grew to include items I seemed to understand a great deal more than the initial set I collected before I was allowed to leave the house.

Today I look in the audience at all of you and I wonder if your passion to reject what I am saying right now is as strong as my passion to reject certain items on spec when I was your age. I really pray that it is because that which is really true will stand up to all attempts to refute it. The stuff that is part of the real Truth will not even render a defense because it does not care. Truth does not care if you believe it. Truth does not care if you like it or hate it. The truth is the truth. Everything else is what people do in an effort to get credit for something. These things would include loudly telling lies.

Persuasion is the application of directional energy on a target body. The certainty of success lies in the knowledge of the spectral profile of the target body. The traditional paradigm of a political campaign is the campaign's ability to persuade various groups that their support is in everyone's best interests and to the detriment of the other campaigns competing for the same office. I have intentionally avoided any mention of the reason for persuasion because our reasons have nothing to do with the results. Our reasons can affect the results as being part of the energy that is applied, but the outcome is the outcome.

I stand here today telling you that I would not be standing here today if I accepted what I was told growing up as being the truth. The reason everything is the way that it is lies in all of the things people chose to believe that were true and were really not true at all. Governments come and go because voters were persuaded to believe things that were apparently not as true as one might have wanted them to be. A case could be made that the bigger the promise, the bigger the lie. The converse being no promises, no lies. The paradox is "How can I promise you that I will make no promises?"

Thank you.

End of Lecture

Fujiwhara Beach City Council Meeting

Pursuant to Public Notice, Mayor FicChaTwentySeven convened a regular meeting of the City Council in the Council Chamber. Those present were

```
Mayor FicChaTwentySeven,

Vice-Mayor FicChaTwentySix,

Councilwoman FicChaThirty,

Councilwoman FicChaTwenty,

Councilman FicChaTwoA,

City Attorney FicChaTwentyThree,

And City Manager FicChaTwoBee.
```

The mayor led a moment of silence and the Pledge of Allegiance.

FicChaTwoBee reported that the recreation department was successful in coming to an agreement with an organization funded by the Florida Department of Elder Affairs, at no charge to the city or the attendees, to assist the elderly with their Medicare, Medicaid, and health insurance questions. She then reported that the insurance industry ratings for the city are now a class one for single and two family homes, but failed to mention the rash of threatened cancellation notices compelled by a data dump of permitting requests for roofing the last fifteen years. If your address was not on that list, you got a letter. If your permit request wasn't within the last five years, someone came by your home to perform an inspection. Then you got a letter. She finished her report by summarizing the distribution of posters declaring Constitution Week as a week of volunteer service.

The first issue to be taken up by the council for consideration was the decision to reduce their liability insurance from five million to two million dollars under the guise of saving money on premiums, which on the surface sounds like a good thing. However, what is not discussed in the light of day is that the Insurance Commissioner, with the support of the Republican held Senate, House of Representatives, and the Governor, negotiated a complex deal towards arbitration requirements by a state licensed arbiter whose job was to keep the matter outside the courtroom and less than or equal to the maximum level of two million dollars. The fix was in as far as process. File an adequate supply of paperwork with the appropriate government offices in order to secure an appointment where you are almost guaranteed to walk out of the room with something. The cap on payments reduced the risk assumed by the insurance companies and the resulting premiums were based on an estimated twenty two percent Earnings Before Taxes and Depreciation.

FicChaTwenty	I make a motion that we approve the proposed course of action as submitted.
FicChaTwentySix	I second the motion.
FicChaTwentySeven	A motion has been made and seconded. I call for a vote. I vote "Aye"
FicChaTwentySix	"Aye"
FicChaTwenty	"Aye"
FicChaTwoA	"Aye"
FicChaThirty	"Aye"
FicChaTwentySeven	By unanimous approval, the motion carries. The next item on the agenda is the request for funding a property appraisal

	of the property to the north that was annexed by the Municipal Corporation of Fujiwhara Beach, Florida and controlled by the United States Air Force in order to share the expense of an upgraded storm water system.
FicChaThirty	We should not spend another red cent on any action that entrenches the Municipal Corporation further into this deal.
FicChaTwentySix	We cannot continue to do nothing and we will not retreat from this long term vision for the city. If we have to spend as much as twenty times more than is currently being requested, it is a bargain.
FicChaThirty	How do you justify that math? It is twelve percent increase in residential Ad Valorem Revenue and a twenty five percent increase in geographical considerations which is estimated to increase the net budget requirements to meet operational needs by sixteen percent. So whether something magical were to happen today and we could begin to collect all that revenue, the Municipal Corporation would be losing money. Compounding the strain is the money that has already been spent and any money that will be spent to continue down this money losing path.
FicChaTwentySix	I make a motion that we approve the funding request as submitted.
FicChaTwenty	I second the motion.

FicChaTwentySeven	A motion has been made and seconded. I call for a vote. I vote "Aye"
FicChaTwentySix	"Aye"
FicChaTwenty	"Aye"
FicChaTwoA	"Aye"
FicChaThirty	"Nay"
FicChaTwentySeven	The motion carries. The next item on the agenda is the resolution relation to prevent elder injuries and falls.

The Fall Prevention Initiative was first conceived as a means to bolster demand for licensed paramedics in heavily unionized regions. The basic tact was to report a set of statistic to which senior citizens could better appreciate the constant peril they were under and be amenable to the idea of your friendly neighborhood paramedic is there for you, so don't worry. The entire plan worked to perfection. The old people, i.e. the people who always vote, want to do what they want to do and society at large owes it to them that they can. The middle aged generation, i.e. the generation whose parents are the old people, are relieved that they can live the life of their dreams with no concern because the government is on the job. So an opportunity is presented for the (god/government/party/candidate) salesman to promise that words will be written and signed into law ensuring that old people can sever their ties with their families and everybody wins. The words allow for partial funding of the program and the local community has to come up with the rest.

The statistics show that old people who live in Fujiwhara Beach are predominantly seasonal such that the normal family support is outside the radius of effectivity. The words written by the federal government provide funds that the states may use to respond to this national danger. The words written by the states accept that money and the conditions to staff openings using registered and state licensed personnel then writes some more words to allow any county or municipal government to apply for some of the money provided that the total estimated cost of implementation is at least twenty five percent greater than the amount being requested. The program is being sold to the voters in Fujiwhara Beach as a godsend from the federal government that makes it possible to take care of our most cherished and fragile citizens.

At this point, the reader may be starting to form some conclusions about where the writer is going with all this. Please allow me the opportunity to finish my thought and then do as you wish.

My question pertains to the expectation that any aspect of personal behavior is to be subsidized in any way by the people who seize our assets. This question leads me to ponder the motivation of a person who arrives at the place where such a subsidy is a good idea when community bonds based on personal accountability and care are weakened. Fujiwhara Beach is a government run retirement center, day care, home owners association and data collection center for the higher levels of government and the industries they regulate. But it's cool, that is what we have been working towards as a group for some time.

FicChaTwenty	I make a motion that we approve the resolution as submitted.
FicChaTwentySix	I second the motion.
FicChaTwentySeven	A motion has been made and seconded. I call for a vote. I vote "Aye"
FicChaTwentySix	"Aye"

FicChaTwenty	"Aye"
FicChaTwoA	"Aye"
FicChaThirty	"Aye"
FicChaTwentySeven	By unanimous approval, the motion carries. The next item on the agenda is approval of the City Employees recommendations for Citizen of the Year, Volunteer of the Year, Organization of the Year, and Business of the Year.

This is one of those agenda items intended to convey the love of the government to those who have demonstrated they are worthy. This year's nominees are the same nominees that get put forward most of the recent past years. The merits of the nominations are communicated through the filters of time, words, or dollars to various causes. The ones who consistently win are the ones who either command the loyalty of the royal court or are being singled out as way to show how magnanimous the gods can be. Or it is just harmless fun and the list was approved without dissent. Since it was the last item on the agenda, the meeting was adjourned and everybody got home in time to watch the newest episode of South Park.

Election Day minus 46 days

Weather Report Fujiwhara Beach, FL

Actual	Avg.	Record	
Mean Temperature	82 °F		
Max Temperature	87 °F	84 °F	93 °F (2006)
Min Temperature	78 °F	75 °F	71 °F (2007)
Dew Point	71 °F		
Average Humidity	68		
Maximum Humidity	81		
Minimum Humidity	58		
Precipitation	0.00 in		
Sea Level Pressure	30.03 in		
Wind Speed	14 mph (ENE)		
Max Wind Speed	16 mph		
Max Gust Speed	-		
Visibility	10 miles		
Events	None		

Pontification of the MickBill - Religious Tolerance

Cue Music.

Announcer	And now, this week's edition of Pontification of the MickBill.

I believe in one God, creator of all that is seen and unseen. There is more to my beliefs, but the crux of the matter is that my spiritual makeup is an individual thing that has evolved over time and will likely keep evolving. There are others who believe much of the same stuff I believe, but not all of it. There are people who believe things totally contrary to what I believe. Each day, throughout the week, and over the course of the year, we will do things intended to celebrate what we believe. For me to expect anybody else to celebrate at the same time or in the same way as I do seems to create an environment that gets in the way of creating utopia. Anybody who expects me to celebrate at the same time or in the same way as they do gets in the way of creating utopia. A religion that demands conversion or crushing of the "infidels" or non-believers seems to get in the way of creating utopia.

I have often been perplexed by individuals who insist I believe in what they believe, and are disappointed in individuals who become militant or fearful in the presence of a dissimilar belief system. The question I find myself asking is "What kind of god is worth worshipping, if that god could become offended?" The second question I find myself asking is "Why would someone worship a god that experiences the same petty emotions as I am inclined to experience?" The net result of my reactions and questioning is that organized religion, in all its current manifestations, is for people who cannot think for themselves. But just because I might conclude that religious people are small minded, doesn't mean religious people cannot be contributing elements to the America of my dreams. As long as they don't mandate that I become small minded, I won't mandate that they grow up and think for themselves. The one common element to all religions is that individual belief in God is more important than anything else. All the stuff about conversion, spreading the word, and smiting entered into the equation when economics was considered.

In my America, people are free to believe anything they want to believe but no one will be given special consideration because they believe a certain thing. All revenues that exceed expenses will be taxed as profit. All actions that deny an individual's right to pursue life and liberty will be treated as crimes. All references to a deity in the various oaths that are part of our society will be removed. A person who lies under oath is immediately removed society to be dealt with by his or her deity in the afterlife.

In my America, you are free to choose when and how you worship, but no one is required to make any special consideration for your choice. If your religion mandates you not work on Saturday, my suggestion is that you choose a professional endeavor that does not require showing up to your employer's place of business on Saturday. If your religion mandates you completely cover your face, my suggestion is that you accept that you will not be issued a driver's license or passport and that you will be denied access to certain services that insist you show your face such as air travel and banking. If your religion allows you to beat your wife or have sex with under age children, understand that assault and battery as well as pedophilia are crimes and you will be removed from society to be dealt with by your deity in the afterlife. So believe whatever you want to believe. Just don't expect anyone else to put up with your rituals.

The ultimate expression of religious tolerance is a complete prohibition of enforcing any religious view on anyone else or extending any special privileges. To do so would be criminal and result in the removal from society in such a way that you would be dealt with by your deity in the afterlife. Churches, temples, mosques, faith centers, and any other faith based organization would be free to exist but would be treated in the same manner as all revenue generating entities in that money earned is income and anything left over after expenses are paid is taxable profit.

The God that I worship doesn't care about the minutia that people believe their god cares about because the God I worship is the creator of all things, seen and unseen. When aligned with God's energy, wonderful things happen in my life and I am at peace. I stub my toe, get into arguments, and experience unpleasant emotions when I am misaligned with God's energy. Either way, the God I worship just keeps on keeping on.

Cue Music.

Announcer	This has been a Pontification of the MickBill.
Producer	And we're out.

Election Day minus 45 days

Weather Report Fujiwhara Beach, FL			
Actual	Avg.	Record	
Mean Temperature	79 °F		
Max Temperature	80 °F	84 °F	89 °F (2002)
Min Temperature	79 °F	75 °F	57 °F (1999)
Dew Point	66 °F		
Average Humidity	64		
Maximum Humidity	66		
Minimum Humidity	62		
Precipitation	0.00 in		
Sea Level Pressure	30.01 in		
Wind Speed	11 mph (ENE)		
Max Wind Speed	13 mph		
Max Gust Speed	-		
Visibility	10 miles		
Events	None		

That Saturday Morning

TGTDTT	I've been thinking.
MickBill	Why do you tell me that? Am I supposed to be affected by that somehow? Is it an announcement on par with "I pooped my pants."?
TGTDTT	Now that you mention it, my drawers do feel kind of squishy. I want FicChaTwelve to win the Florida Senate District 16 seat in the General Election.
ShugaJoel	His wife would never let that happen.
TGTDTT	His wife has no choice unless he withdraws from the race. I believe that deep down inside, FicChaTwelve wants to see his name displayed one more time on election night. I think he sees it as something his grandkids can brag about.
ShugaJoel	Again, his wife would never let that happen.
TGTDTT	I do not believe that either of them would ever have to know until the election results are announced. Is there somebody else you trust more than FicChaTwelve? Talk about a guy who would take a bullet.
MickBill	How would we do this?
ShugaJoel	I am going to start by pretending we never had this conversation and then move on to eating my breakfast.

Election Day minus 44 days

Weather Report where the Committee meets

Actual	Avg.	Record	
Mean Temperature	72 °F	69 °F	
Max Temperature	80 °F	78 °F	96 °F (1895)
Min Temperature	64 °F	61 °F	41 °F (1956)
Dew Point	62 °F		
Average Humidity	72		
Maximum Humidity	90		
Minimum Humidity	54		
Precipitation	0.87 in	0.13 in	2.18 (1979)
Sea Level Pressure	29.80 in		
Wind Speed	10 mph (SSW)		
Max Wind Speed	20 mph		
Max Gust Speed	25 mph		
Visibility	7 miles		
Events	Rain		

Homeland Security Summary to Committee

- Population deemed subversive to government remain within current guidelines if a Phase 1 lockdown were required.

- Eighty two out of one hundred voters align themselves with the current two party electoral system.

- The nationalization of industries abroad have exposed weaknesses in the control of sensitive information transmitted over the air or through a network.

- Threats of force to government are numerous. The extent of the threats is unknown.

- The single biggest threat to government is the upcoming nationwide election. It is possible, but not likely that independent candidates could replace party affiliated candidates in many critical offices.

Committee Meeting

What do we expect things to look like the day after?

Three	The most recent forecast shows a continued rise in the transition from the two recognized political parties to independent status tracks adjusted viewership of The Dr. Charles Lectures.
Two	Why adjusted viewership?
Three	It is adjusted to account for the people who have been watching the videos. A person who has already made the transition to Independent status is excluded from the model.
Five	Is that done algorithmically or statistically?
Three	Both, actually. Since the data feeding into forecast model is constantly updated, the model quantifies the error of the prediction to the latest data sets as well as optimizes the coefficients in the prediction process.
Four	And to think that I know people who still think people should take a civics course instead of an Algebra course.
One	How high do we expect the tidal surge to be?
Three	On the day of implementation, six more lectures are scheduled to have been given. The impact seems to be in the six million

more range. It is more than we have ever seen but it is less than what would be needed for anything drastic to happen.

One — I hope you are right.

Election Day minus 41 days

Weather Report Northfield, VT

Actual	Avg.	Record	
Mean Temperature	50 °F	54 °F	
Max Temperature	57 °F	65 °F	83 °F (1961)
Min Temperature	43 °F	43 °F	20 °F (1963)
Dew Point	39 °F		
Average Humidity	70		
Maximum Humidity	86		
Minimum Humidity	54		
Precipitation	0.00 in	0.12 in	1.08 (1965)
Sea Level Pressure	30.01 in		
Wind Speed	6 mph (NW)		
Max Wind Speed	21 mph		
Max Gust Speed	25 mph		
Visibility	10 miles		
Events	None		

The Dr. Charles Lectures - Curses of the Human Condition

POL4350 – Political Absolutes Lecture 8

Professor Bailey Charles

Dr. Charles

It is about this time in the semester that students typically begin to bore of my opening remarks that I am a committed liar. You are free to feel as you choose to feel. But if I am going to give a lecture, I want to make absolutely certain that if someone learns something valuable, they did not learn it from me. All I ever did was lie to every student I have ever spoken to and I am not going to stop lying now.

Let us get started.

It seems to be somewhat true that the curse of the human condition manifests itself in three interconnected ways:

1. Self-Awareness – the idea that you and I are separate from each other. This idea includes the absence of a real and tangible connection to God.

2. Memory – our tendency to poorly record the information associated with some experience and our physiological response.

3. The Ability to Count – the allowance for the flawed idea that repetitive events

must be an ever-increasing function with respect to its perceived quality or benefit.

Of the items listed above, dealing with item 1 gives me the most running room in terms of dealing with the fact that I am still here. Not only does item 1 open the channels for understanding what I was intended here for, but it renders items 2 and 3 meaningless. I will still have a memory and I will still be able to count, but those things will no longer impede my capacity to manifest God's intention through my own life.

When I am alone, I lose my self-awareness to a degree that is connected to the thoughts I am having about all of the relationships in my life. These thoughts eventually morph into a loosely constructed compare and contrast.

Over the course of my life, the mechanism by which I compare and contrast has evolved, but it still yields product that keeps me from understanding what I was intended to understand.

As long I think I have a thought that makes a point that you are unaware of, I am a human being that is just as screwed up as you are.

But there are moments when I have no such thoughts. There are moments when I am filled with inspiration to do something truly wonderful.

As soon as I begin to understand that I am having such a moment, my attention turns towards how I would go about doing it. Then I start to wonder how I might be able to get you to give me money to do it. Then I start wondering how much money I might be able to get you to give me. Then I start thinking about what I would do with that money. Then I can't remember what the idea was in the first place.

Thank you.

End of Lecture

Election Day minus 39 days

Weather Report Fujiwhara Beach, FL

Actual	Avg.	Record	
Mean Temperature	84 °F		
Max Temperature	91 °F	83 °F	91 °F (2013)
Min Temperature	76 °F	74 °F	69 °F (2008)
Dew Point	73 °F		
Average Humidity	77		
Maximum Humidity	94		
Minimum Humidity	46		
Precipitation	0.00 in		
Sea Level Pressure	29.83 in		
Wind Speed	13 mph (WNW)		
Max Wind Speed	22 mph		
Max Gust Speed	-		
Visibility	10 miles		
Events	None		

Pontification of the MickBill - Secular Rule

Cue Music.

Announcer	And now, this week's edition of Pontification of the MickBill.

In my America, there is only one crime and that crime is theft. The response to someone convicted of theft is their immediate removal in such a way that the individual would be dealt with by the deity of their choice in the afterlife. Imprisonment would be implemented only during the initial arrest and trial stage. There would be no bail and no appeal. If a person were found guilty of theft, the sentence would be carried out immediately and with no ceremony. Examples of how various acts currently considered illegal are really theft:

- Theft of any kind is theft.
- Murder is theft of a person's life.
- Rape is theft of a person's body.
- Pedophilia and child pornography are theft of a child's innocence.
- Driving under the influence of alcohol or drugs, road-rage, and wreck less driving are theft of the public's safety.
- Identity-theft is theft of a person's individuality and financial records.
- Stock fraud, Ponzi schemes, and insider trading are theft of a free market capitalistic system.

- Breaking and Entry, including trespassing, is theft of a person's right to privacy and the sanctity of their home or business.

- Vandalism, including graffiti, is the theft of a person's property rights.

- Perjury and other false official statements are theft of a community's right to know the truth.

- Manufacture and/or sale of controlled non-naturally occurring substances without a license is theft of a public's right to have assurances of safe products.

- Sale or distribution of a controlled substance, naturally occurring or not, to a minor is theft of a child's ability to develop naturally and a parent's right to guide that development.

- Tax evasion is theft from the society.

- Knowingly providing aid and/or shelter to someone who has committed a crime is just lame.

The above list is not all-inclusive, but it is sufficient to clearly establish the philosophical framework to guide personal behavior and provide relief for an over-burdened judicial system. But we still need to give thought to some of the actions that are considered illegal today but would become legal in the America of my dreams.

The most prominent example of something that would become legal is the possession and cultivation of marijuana for individual and private use. My reasoning here is that there is no way to reasonably establish that a person who grows marijuana in the privacy of their own home and smokes it themselves causes anybody any problems. If the person operates a vehicle while under the influence, we will have a penalty for that. If the person sells it to an adult and fails to report the income, we have a penalty for that. Pick any of the concerns associated with marijuana use and you will see the aforementioned list deals with the problem, if it is a real problem.

Another example of something that would become legal is prostitution. Two consenting adults engaging in a sexual act for a fee cannot be framed in a manner that can be shown as one person stealing from another. If either person is a minor, we have that covered. The rest falls under the category of decency and personal choice, which cannot be legislated without infringing on the Constitution of the United States of America.

The net effect of my vision is that there will be a few things that are illegal and dealt with by the permanent removal from society and everything else will be legal. This means that an employer has the legal right to only employ people who are not nude in public. The employer will also have the right to insist their employees remain drug free and that drug tests, as conditions of employment, are perfectly acceptable. My approach also means that helmet and seat belt laws are unconstitutional but insurance companies have the right to refrain from covering a person who does not wear a helmet while riding a motorcycle or a seatbelt while driving. Civil and Traffic Courts will handle everything else that cannot be defined in terms of theft.

From a practical point of view, the population of the United States of America currently exceeds its capacity for employment on the order of twenty percent, which means we have an excess inventory of employable people and our prison system continues to grow in order to meet the demand caused by repeat offenders and those who will never be released. The bottom line is that we can afford to thin the heard. If we do it right, the cost of our justice system will reduce, prison over-crowding will become a thing of the past, and people will live their lives with a little more respect for others if they wish to live their lives at all.

Just to get the ball rolling, my mentioning of permanently removing people, is execution. The methods we currently use and the system that implements it are expensive, cumbersome, barbaric, and flawed. The method I propose is inexpensive and, by all accounts, painless. The system I propose is straightforward.

The method is nothing more than a shot or drink of a solution that induces sleep followed by a 30-minute session breathing carbon monoxide gas from a mask. At today's prices, the entire process will cost less than two hundred dollars, including security personnel and everything I have been able to find out about carbon monoxide poisoning leads me to believe it is one hundred percent effective and completely painless.

The system I have in mind is simple in that a jury convicts or acquits an individual of theft with the clear understanding that an acquittal means freedom and a conviction means permanent removal from society. There is no in-between or sense of punishment fitting a crime. It has to be that cut and dry so that everybody is responsible for what they do and understands that responsibility. Adults and minors are subjected to the same process without exception. If a person is convicted of doing something that reduces the safety and security of law-abiding citizens, they are immediately and permanently removed.

Cue Music.

Announcer	This has been a Pontification of the MickBill.
Producer	And we're out.

Election Day minus 38 Days

Weather Report Fujiwhara Beach, FL

Actual	Avg.	Record	
Mean Temperature	78 °F		
Max Temperature	83 °F	83 °F	93 °F (2002)
Min Temperature	72 °F	74 °F	72 °F (2008)
Dew Point	71 °F		
Average Humidity	82		
Maximum Humidity	92		
Minimum Humidity	66		
Precipitation	0.38 in		
Sea Level Pressure	29.91 in		
Wind Speed	10 mph (NNE)		
Max Wind Speed	20 mph		
Max Gust Speed	25 mph		
Visibility	9 miles		
Events	Rain		

That Saturday Morning

Whether everybody is together in one place physically or not is not the real metric for whether a meeting actually took place in today's interconnected society. Between the telephone, cell phones, internet, email, and text messaging a real exchange of ideas can happen and decisions are made that represent the collective thinking of the group.

Unless you think OBandSD, who thinks running an extension cord from his friend's home to the airstream trailer parked in his side yard that he calls his front yard, is too connected to the system, he still believes that you look a person in the eyes when you have something to say to them. If it is not important enough to say to them in person, then it is not important. He doesn't even write letters.

TGTDTT	We all know people who know people.
MickBill	We do.
OBandSD	I know you guys.
ShugaJoel	Exactly what do we tell them?
FicChaTen	We tell them that FicChaTwelve has lived his entire life as a stand-up guy. We tell them that he does not want this gig and the only reason he signed up as a Democratic write in candidate was to keep the Republican Primary closed. We tell them that if there was anybody who did not want to be elected more than FicChaTwelve, I would like to meet them. That is why when they are casting their votes, they should vote for FicChaTwelve. They should tell

their friends to vote for FicChaTwelve. Then we tell them that they should keep quiet about it.

ShugaJoel — This is the most interesting surprise party I have ever imagined.

OBandSD — What are you guys talking about?

FicChaTen — Are you sure you want to know? The last thing you need is to draw the attention of the Fujiwhara Beach Building Inspector.

OBandSD — It seems to me as if each of you have something to lose as well.

TGTDTT — If we say the wrong thing to the wrong person or if we engage for the wrong reasons, we all deserve to lose something.

ShugaJoel — I don't see what there is to gain.

TGTDTT — George Washington did not want the jobs that he was given and he ended up being the model that we use today for the character of the person who most deserves to be president. To a person who just wants to live their life in peace, a call to public service is distasteful. Only the clear in mind and pure in heart will do the job as it is meant to be done. All of these other candidates are saying "Look at me. I am a great person. I can make your world a better place." FicChaTwelve is the only candidate who is not saying any of those things. In fact, he is not saying anything at

	all in the hope that he loses the election and stays under the radar for his family's sake.
MickBill	He will lose the election.
TGTDTT	Why does he have to lose?
MickBill	Nobody who knows he is a candidate believes he is a serious candidate. He has no public support. He has no money. He has no endorsements. He is not making any public statements.
TGTDTT	If you had to make a choice today for the person you trust the most to represent you in the Florida State Senate, you are telling me you would not select FicChaTwelve?
ShugaJoel	It does seem like a wasted vote.
TGTDTT	Why is the vote wasted if it is cast in accordance with the voter's sincerest intentions?
MickBill	Because this is the real world.
TGTDTT	All of us sitting at this table have endeavored our entire lives to create the reality that we imagine. The same is true for every single person we see in this diner and walking around to the other shops. If we can understand that what we now have is our making, we can also understand that we can make our reality something better if we choose to.

MickBill — This is not the time to go off on a flight of fantasy. There are real problems that need solutions and you want to throw a "Hail Mary" that has almost no chance of being caught by the person we want to catch it.

FicChaTen — The district is almost ninety percent Republican. There is no chance he can win.

TGTDTT — That is not true and you know it. I concede the voter registrations line up the way they do. But everybody at this table still has a hard time remembering that FicChaTwleve is a registered Democrat. And I am not taking a flight of fantasy. I am suggesting we find it within our hearts to cast our votes in accordance with our choice and not the expectations of others.

ShugaJoel — I have always done that. Well, not always. When in doubt, I vote Republican. I am not as bad as a buddy of mine who votes Republican no matter what … that's just stupid.

TGTDTT — We all have that buddy or a sister in law who only votes Democrat. That's just as stupid … maybe worse.

MickBill — So what are you suggesting?

OBandSD — TGTDTT is suggesting we must decide for ourselves what is right, to let others know that it is okay for them to do the same.

MickBill — I still don't see how this gets FicChaTwelve elected.

FicChaTen — We let everybody know that it takes six years to completely overhaul all of the elected positions. As long as voters elect people who want the job, they will elect people who have an agenda that ends up hurting everybody but the chosen few. When we elect people who would rather not have the job but are doing it because they were called upon by the people, then government will cease to be as self-serving as it currently is.

Election Day minus 37 Days

Weather Report where the Committee meets

Actual	Avg.	Record	
Mean Temperature	67 °F	66 °F	
Max Temperature	73 °F	75 °F	91 °F (1886)
Min Temperature	60 °F	58 °F	42 °F (1947)
Dew Point	53 °F		
Average Humidity	64		
Maximum Humidity	78		
Minimum Humidity	49		
Precipitation	0.00 in	0.12 in	2.46 (2004)
Sea Level Pressure	30.27 in		
Wind Speed	5 mph (NE)		
Max Wind Speed	13 mph		
Max Gust Speed	17 mph		
Visibility	10 miles		
Events	None		

Homeland Security Summary to Committee

- Population deemed subversive to government remains within current guidelines if a Phase 1 lockdown were required.

- Eighty one out of one hundred voters align themselves with the current two party electoral system.

- The nationalization of industries abroad have exposed weaknesses in the control of sensitive information transmitted over the air or through a network.

- Threats of force to government are numerous. The extent of the threats is unknown.

- The single biggest threat to government is the upcoming nationwide election. It is possible, but not likely that independent candidates could replace party affiliated candidates in many critical offices.

Committee Meeting

Three	Somebody tell me how this all works.
Five	Which part? The part where we find out something is wrong? The part where we think we know why? Or the part where we do something about it?
Three	All of it.
Five	Homeland Security, or more specifically, the National Security Agency, Federal Bureau of Investigation and the Central Intelligence Agency, has been conducting and improving data mining operations since the Cold War. With the widespread use of the internet, data mining has become automated to a large degree. Algorithms to identify particular trends in internet traffic were developed to anticipate potential threats to the government. The Algorithms are typically nothing more than a set of digital filters by which actual data is compared to various theoretical scenarios. For instance, the security of the government depends on the existence of support domestically and an absence of threats internationally. The existence of domestic support can be checked in a number of ways where one of the flags is the percentage of population that is aligned with either of the two major political parties. If the percentage drops below a certain

value than the conclusion is that a revolution is at hand. If the percentage changes, then trend analysis is performed to identify a point in the future where the percentage will drop below a certain value.

Three — What is the percentage?

Five — It is not a set number across the board. It depends on which elected officials are making certain decisions. For instance, we don't care if some back bench do-nothing Democrat or Republican congressman gets replaced by a third party candidate but we do care if the Speaker of the House or the Senate Pro Tem is replaced. We also care if it looks likes the balance of power in one of the houses of congress shifts towards independents. So each elected official has their own threshold.

Three — Then what?

Five — If the math models show a likelihood that an independent majority is possible within four or more election cycles, additional mining is performed to root out the cause based on correlated events. In this case, there is sufficient correlation to identify the Dr. Charles Lectures as being the impetus for change.

Four — How do we know the conclusions are correct?

Two — Every person who works in Homeland Security takes an oath of loyalty to the

	government of the United States of America. They have a vested interest in being correct and we have a vested interest in trusting them.
Four	Vested interest? This has become the standard by which we make life and death choices?
One	Vested interest has always been the standard. Besides, if we deal with the professor and the trend continues, the next most likely cause will become apparent and we will deal with that until the trend reverses.
Three	Homeland Security is looking to us to make a decision right now. We need to tell them what we want them to do.
One	Tell them to respond to the current threat.
Four	This is wrong. Being an independent voter does not make a person a subversive. And a government run by independent candidates is what this nation's founding fathers intended.
Two	Times have changed. The world has changed. We know a great deal more now than the founding fathers did. Besides, with an effective unemployment rate over fifteen percent, we have room for error.
One	We need to give the order.
Five	I already did.

Election Day minus 34 days

Weather Report Northfield, VT			
Actual	Avg.	Record	
Mean Temperature	56 °F	51 °F	
Max Temperature	71 °F	62 °F	79 °F (1950)
Min Temperature	40 °F	40 °F	24 °F (1963)
Dew Point	45 °F		
Average Humidity	75		
Maximum Humidity	100		
Minimum Humidity	49		
Precipitation	0.00 in	0.11 in	3.58 (2010)
Sea Level Pressure	30.02 in		
Wind Speed	2 mph (WSW)		
Max Wind Speed	13 mph		
Max Gust Speed	16 mph		
Visibility	4 miles		
Events	Fog		

The Dr. Charles Lectures - A Considered Question

POL4350 – Political Absolutes Lecture 9

Professor Bailey Charles

Dr. Charles	Tonight I will tell my biggest lies of the semester. Constraining our travels to be a single thread unraveling in time, there are four point six billion years of data points to be considered and each of those data points has at least three hundred and sixty-five data points and each of those data points has at least twenty-four data points. Each of those data points can have at least 3,600 data points. Assuming we want to get to be one with all of it, we are talking about the simultaneous illumination, or re-call, of no fewer than 1.450656e17 data points (1,450,656,000,00000000). If one were to want to assign a single pixel to every data point, the image would be 380,874,783 pixels by 380,874,783 pixels. If each pixel were one square millimeter, the image would be an area 56,010 square miles which is a box about 237 miles on each side. The average person has cognitive periph-eral vision that extends only out to about twenty degrees from the direction a person

is looking. An extremely aware person, especially one who is well practiced in the clandestine or combat arts will respond to visual stimuli approaching, but never reaching a vector that is orthogonal to the line of sight.

Applying trigonometric relationships, substituting the actual values specified above, the average person would have to be about three hundred and twenty five miles away from the image to see it all with a single view. The more aware person is, the closer to the image they can be and still take it all in. Or put another way, the astronauts on the International Space Station can stare out the Cupola and take in an entire hemisphere of the planet rotating before them. The average orbit takes about 90 minutes, but the orbit changes over time.

Let's allow for the possibility that the space station travels in a repeatable fashion such that there is a time, "tn," such that the view from the space station is exactly the same as all "tn" where "n" is equal to integer multiples of the periodicity. The astronaut, separated from his family and life on earth could look down below on his home and see his family.

That can't happen, you say? The first question I have to ask is that if I could just think it up and apply proven techniques to glean some newfound understanding, is this not just the beginning of another advancement in our understanding?

Why should anyone care if an astronaut could actually look down on his or her home from space? The answer lies in the truth that the astronaut will return home one day or will die in space. With every moment the astronaut is in space, those are the only two outcomes of the mission. When the astronaut is busy, there is no time to consider which of the two outcomes is to be theirs. When the astronaut has moments alone, staring out the cupola, there is a chance the astronaut might consider the question and would benefit from a sense of inspiration.

Staring out the window of a ship far away, where the view before you is your life and the only two options you have before you is to return to your life or die out in space, what questions begin to emerge in your mind?

I knew this guy who was a submarine sailor who has gone to sea for months at a time with no cupola from which to stare. He was left with his imagination and thoughts to fill the gaps between doing his job, sleeping, and eating. What he began to learn is that his time away helps him decide what life he intended to lead when he returned to port. In every case, he was looking forward to doing something that he imagined while he was at sea.

It occurred to me that as much fun as dreaming is, the end effect is the build-up of stored energy that gets released when he went on liberty. The longer he was at sea, the more energy he released when he got back to port.

Then one day, he stopped going to sea. It took him a while to adjust his relationships with Terra Firma and those in his life. He learned that he cannot be on liberty every day and he must have moments where he can "go to sea" so that he is a renewed and wiser person when he returns. What he described has many names. Prayer and meditation are the two more commonly used. But that is what it is.

He found that if he could frame his goals in such a way that it was worth paying the ultimate price to achieve them, then any failure in his life was honorable. If he could not frame his goals in such a way, then reaching the goal was always the result of a less-than one hundred percent effort. Where is the fun in that?

I had a thing that was worth a thing and I very much wanted at least one new thing that was worth the same thing as the thing I no longer have. In other words: Seek out and identify at least one target suitable for the only weapons in your arsenal. Try not to be wasteful.

I must do something worthy of expending my last breath doing. I must do something that is worth risking everything else in my life for. I must die the death of a soldier in battle and be worthy of the highest praise. If I am not willing to do that, then I best sit down and shut up unless someone asks me what I think. But until someone asks me something, I had best be using my time for something of even remote value to me.

Things that seem to inspire the most desirable of responses are those things that cause me to laugh uncontrollably or cry uncontrollably. Examples include performing the music as I imagine it to be in that moment or handling the jib sheets while out on "Big Blue" and its blowing twenty knots with gusts up to thirty in eight feet of choppy seas. I will let you guess which of these makes me laugh and which makes me cry.

Both of these examples are self-centered in that I give no mention as to how either of these two things benefits the greater good. My counter argument is that one would be hard pressed how my achieving nirvana in both those instances does anything but make this a better place to be. We all know what it is like to watch others try to act like they are in the moment. When we witness it in person, we can almost see the person crying out their fear that they will be discovered as acting. But every now and then, we get to witness first hand a real person giving it their all in a real life situation. The ultimate experience is being the person giving it all they have in a real life situation.

There is a time and a place for the big stuff like a live performance or a sailing regatta, but every moment of every day is an opportunity to do something cool. The more stuff we think is cool, the more stuff we'll do. When there are times when I am unable to think of anything cool that I can do on my own, I start reaching out to people I know to ask them if there is anything I can do to be of help to them.

There countless examples in texts, both ancient and modern, that praises the benefits of an active life that serves the good of others. There are an equal number of examples when the action is not balanced with a certain amount of reflection, rest, and selfishness.

But if one had to choose an extreme of activity with no distraction or complete inactivity, the seemingly better choice is that of activity. When our efforts become totally internal, we become nothing more than an absorber of the energy around us.

In the extreme case, we might be talking about individuals who defraud the welfare systems that our various governments have in place. We are definitely talking about the people who pass laws for the purpose of being re-elected. These two groups do far more damage to the world than all the people who enjoy sailing and playing music ever could.

A far more considered question would concern a person's actions and not some label they have unnecessarily been assigned. Labels assigned to us by others and those we assign ourselves.

Thank you.

End of Lecture

Fujiwhara Beach City Council Meeting

Pursuant to Public Notice, Mayor FicChaTwentySeven convened a regular meeting of the City Council in the Council Chamber. Those present were

```
Mayor FicChaTwentySeven,

Vice-Mayor FicChaTwentySix,

Councilwoman FicChaThirty,

Councilwoman FicChaTwenty,

Councilman FicChaTwoA,

City Attorney FicChaTwentyThree,

And City Manager FicChaTwoBee.
```

The mayor led a moment of silence and the Pledge of Allegiance.

FicChaTwoBee reported that the Municipal Corporation of Fujiwhara Beach is fully compliant with the current understanding of the requirements set forth by the Affordable Care Act. She further reported that the Federal Emergency Management Agency has given the 'go' for the revised Flood Plain Management Ordinance. Her report ended with the announcement that the City-run community center will host a mass flu vaccination to be conducted by the Visiting Nurses Association. Her next report caused some discussion.

FicChaTwoBee	The County has cut their budget for first responders and they reimburse us for the loaded cost of one junior patrol officer or firefighter. That money is gone. It is easier to lose a junior patrol officer than a member of

a firefighting crew. I have already informed the Police Chief.

FicChaThirty — Our staffing levels have always been budget driven and not need driven, which makes me think there is something that you know that you are not telling us.

FicChaTwentySeven — Thank you FicChaTwoBee. The first item on the agenda is whether we allow the moratorium on enforcement of the city codes prohibiting the temporary signage.

FicChaTwenty — I make a motion that we allow the moratorium to expire and resume enforcement of all city codes.

FicChaTwentySix — I second the motion.

FicChaTwentySeven — A motion has been made and seconded. I call for a vote. I vote "Aye"

FicChaTwentySix — "Aye"

FicChaTwenty — "Aye"

FicChaTwoA — "Aye"

FicChaThirty — "Nay"

FicChaTwentySeven — The "Ayes" have it. The motion carries. The next item on the agenda is the approval of the revised City Council Policies and Procedures.

FicChaThirty	I just want to say that I love the changes FicChaTwenty has made to the policies and procedures. It is an extremely powerful means to suppress dissent. I especially love the part where a city employee can choose whether to answer a question from a council member or whether to provide the requested data. Very transparent!
FicChaTwenty	The staff is here to run the city, not to be your personal research assistants. I make a motion we approve the revised City Council Policies and Procedures.
FicChaTwentySix	I second the motion.
FicChaTwentySeven	A motion has been made and seconded. I call for a vote. I vote "Aye"
FicChaTwentySix	"Aye"
FicChaTwenty	"Aye"
FicChaTwoA	"Aye"
FicChaThirty	"Nay"
FicChaTwentySeven	The "Ayes" have it. The motion carries. The next item on the agenda is Illicit Discharge Ordinance that we must pass or we will be in violation of state and federal law.
FicChaTwentySix	I make the motion we approve the law that we have to approve in order to be compliant with laws passed by the higher gods.

FicChaTwoA	I want to second this one.
FicChaTwentySeven	A motion has been made and seconded. I call for a vote. I vote "Aye"
FicChaTwentySix	"Aye"
FicChaTwenty	"Aye"
FicChaTwoA	"Aye"
FicChaThirty	"Nay"
FicChaTwentySeven	The "Ayes" have it. The motion carries. That was the last item on the agenda. This meeting is adjourned.

Election Day minus 32 days

Weather Report Fujiwhara Beach, FL			
Actual	Avg.	Record	
Mean Temperature	82 °F		
Max Temperature	86 °F	82 °F	87 °F (2012)
Min Temperature	78 °F	74 °F	69 °F (2001)
Dew Point	69 °F		
Average Humidity	66		
Maximum Humidity	72		
Minimum Humidity	58		
Precipitation	0.00 in		
Sea Level Pressure	30.06 in		
Wind Speed	7 mph (East)		
Max Wind Speed	10 mph		
Max Gust Speed	-		
Visibility	10 miles		
Events	None		

Pontification of the MickBill - Vested Interests

Cue Music.

Announcer	And now, this week's edition of Pontification of the MickBill.

To me, the idea of vested interest speaks to our innate tendency towards self-preservation. In the extreme, "vested interest" is selfishness. The idea of doing things that benefit ourselves is not necessarily a bad thing because there are some things that we all need. Often we can do things that help ourselves and others. For instance, building my home in such a way that I use the water that comes from the rain instead of the water that comes from the city, my water bill is lower and there is more water available for others. If I invest in windmills and solar panels so that my electric bill is lower, it benefits everybody through a reduced demand on the power grid and the people who make solar panels and windmills have jobs.

What experience has taught me is that when I have done something for the purpose of helping someone else and I could not see how it also helped me, my actions backfired. The phrase "No good deed goes unpunished." has rung true more times than I care to remember. Those who do such things are often called martyrs and it is rare that a martyr ever accomplishes something that makes the world a better place. More often than not, their personal sacrifice had no real effect on the outcome. The life of Sister Theresa and all of her charitable works has had no discernible impact on alleviating poverty and suffering in the world. I believe that Sister Theresa was a good person and deserves the honors and adoration that comes with being canonized a saint, but I don't believe she solved a single problem. Gandhi, on the other hand did solve a problem that benefited him and others. His assassination was not an act of martyrdom but the reality of living in a world with small-minded people. The same is true of Martin Luther King, Jr. and Malcolm X.

In the America I dream of, people would stop being crusaders and martyrs and instead engage in activities that benefit themselves and potentially others. At the very least, people would engage in activities that benefit themselves and not harm others. An economy based on "vested interest" tends to be more vibrant and robust. All one has to do is look at the dismal failures of the various socialist nations to have an appreciation for capitalism. In the America of my dreams, philanthropy would be an individual effort within the private sector and each initiative would be framed as serving a personal and vested interest.

In some way I am giving voice to my frustration with individuals who wear those rubber wristbands or ribbons in order to promote one of the infinite causes in our society and throughout the world. All of these people who do this, as well as host telethons or star on public service announcements are making an ill-fated attempt to address, not only their own irrelevance, but their hypocrisy by telling all of us that we are not doing what we can to make the world a better place and that we should somehow feel guilty. I submit that these people are not putting their talents to their best use in order to solve any of the problems they speak about. They are merely doing what they want to do to promote their own image and attempt to convince themselves and others that their existence has meaning. If you think I am off base, pick any television spokesman and the cause they support and check to see whether there has been any tangible progress to elimination of the problem. The greatest advancements in science have never been the result of a telethon or public service announcement. The advancements were the result of hard work by countless people, some of whom became famous later but none of them became famous prior to the discovery or accomplishment.

In the America I dream of, everybody will be doing everything they can as individuals to be happy and make the world a better place instead of wearing ribbons or bracelets and telling everybody else they need to do more. In the America of my dreams, people will ask for help when they need help accomplishing something important to them and limit their requests to those that they are directly involved with.

Cue Music.

Announcer	This has been a Pontification of the MickBill.
Producer	And we're out.

Election Day minus 31 Days

Weather Report Fujiwhara Beach, FL

Actual	Avg.	Record		
Mean Temperature	82 °F			
Max Temperature	85 °F	82 °F	87 °F (2012)	
Min Temperature	78 °F	73 °F	71 °F (2010)	
Dew Point	69 °F			
Average Humidity	67			
Maximum Humidity	73			
Minimum Humidity	60			
Precipitation	0.00 in			
Sea Level Pressure	30.07 in			
Wind Speed	7 mph (ENE)			
Max Wind Speed	12 mph			
Max Gust Speed	-			
Visibility	10 miles			
Events	None			

That Saturday Morning

TGTDTT I keep wondering how the last election turned out the way that it did. How did FicChaTwenty, with her committed liberal tendencies win a seat on the Fujiwhara Beach City Council when the city went sixty percent for the Republican in the Presidential Election … especially with the achievements made by the "New Kids" council in their short 11 months?

OBandSD Maybe it really didn't, but the reported results made it look that way.

MickBill A municipality can choose to manage its own elections.

ShugaJoel Don't even go there. Our elections are the last vestige of a civilized society. I refuse to allow for the possibility that the local elections were rigged.

FicChaTen If they were, it would certainly make the results make sense.

TGTDTT Who is watching the watchers? But that particular election was run by the County Elections Supervisor.

MickBill Do you know how many volunteers get used during the early voting and Election Day activities? Not to mention people who are part time and only work during the election season?

OBandSD — My grandfather made some money betting on the 1918 World Series. When I would talk to him about betting on games, he would say he never gambled. I remembered FicChaTwenty spending a great deal of time in hushed conversations with the City Clerk before the election. I also remember the look on the City Clerk's face when the conversation was over. At the time, I thought something different. But now I am not so sure.

FicChaTen — So what do we do?

TGTDTT — There is nothing we can do, but it explains why poll monitors and elected officials have an important role to play.

FicChaTen — But is it a role they play ethically?

MickBill — I will vouch for our elections Supervisor with my life. Don't you dare drag her into this.

TGTDTT — How could the Fujiwhara Beach City Council results have been falsified in an election being run by the county?

FicChaTen — Control who gets in the room. Control what happens in the room. Control what is said and posted afterwards.

OBandSD — That is a lot of control to be counting on. One approach is to change the ballots during the transit from the precinct to where they would be counted. Another approach is to the change the software that counts the ballots. The last place is to change the results. Knowing what I know about some of the people involved, I would bet that the results were changed. There is no way to swap all the ballots and to get the software changed without the change getting flagged seems too far-fetched.

MickBill I am not letting any of you take me down this path. FicChaTwelve lost the race and that is all there is too it.

ShugaJoel I am with you there.

TGTDTT You two are right. Are we getting off track?

FicChaTen We got off track a long time ago.

TGTDTT I have sent an email to every person that I know announcing that I will not discuss the upcoming election and I will be voting for the people who are committed to getting government as far away from my everyday life as humanly possible. I then asked them to consider doing the same.

ShugaJoel You didn't mention FicChaTwelve?

TGTDTT I want people thinking right now. If we give them a name then the opposition starts. It would be best if we gave the people something to wrestle with the idea that the choice they make in the voting booth is between them and God. Nobody else needs to know who a person voted for.

ShugaJoel	So how do we get them to think about FicChaTwelve? His name will not even be on the ballot. People will have to write his name in if they intend to vote for him.
MickBill	I asked FicChaTwelve to come on the show and he won't do it. I guess I could make something out of that on the air.
OBandSD	You all are trying to plan, strategize, and prepare so that the voters are where we want them to be on Election Day. Please tell me you know who you sound like right now.
FicChaTen	We have to do something and this is too important to do wrong.
TGTDTT	Then go do something correctly. But do it on your own because you believe it is the right thing to do. If you don't do something because you don't think we want you to then you are as lost as the person that does something because he thinks other people want him to do it.
FicChaTen	We need a plan.
TGTDTT	I have a plan. My plan has me doing and saying what I think I should do and say while ignoring what others are telling me to do or say. The difference between my plan and any plan you want us to come up with is that your plan will cause one or more of us to make a choice for a known wrong reason, my plan will have me making

choices with a chance I will make them for the right reasons.

FicChaTen	You are such a purest.
TGTDTT	I am just the guy that does the thing.

Election Day minus 30 Days

Weather Report where the Committee meets

Actual	Avg.	Record	
Mean Temperature	79 °F	63 °F	
Max Temperature	89 °F	72 °F	96 °F (1941)
Min Temperature	69 °F	55 °F	37 °F (1935)
Dew Point	66 °F		
Average Humidity	67		
Maximum Humidity	90		
Minimum Humidity	43		
Precipitation	0.00 in	0.11 in	2.53 (1932)
Sea Level Pressure	30.06 in		
Wind Speed	5 mph (South)		
Max Wind Speed	12 mph		
Max Gust Speed	14 mph		
Visibility	10 miles		
Events	None		

Homeland Security Summary to Committee

- Population deemed subversive to government remains within current guidelines if a Phase 1 lockdown were required.

- Eighty out of one hundred voters align themselves with the current two party electoral system.

- The nationalization of industries abroad have exposed weaknesses in the control of sensitive information transmitted over the air or through a network.

- Threats of force to government are numerous. The extent of the threats is unknown.

- The single biggest threat to government is the upcoming nationwide election. It is possible, but not likely that independent candidates could replace party affiliated candidates in many critical offices.

Committee Meeting

Four	Tell me again why this is a problem.
One	For over 300 years this committee has guided the unruly masses to a civilization that battles foreign nations but not itself. If the people no longer heed the counsel of this committee then the people are likely to turn on each other.
Two	And we are out of a job.
Four	Is your concern that we are out of a job or the people will kill each other?
Three	Both. It almost happened in the very beginning during the Whiskey Rebellion. It happened again in the 1860's, again the 1920's, 1960's, and 70's.
Five	In each of those periods it was necessary to use force on a large scale until order was restored.
Four	So now we think we know enough to identify how to squash these rebellions in a way that no one will notice.
Five	Now you are starting to understand.
Four	Is it possible that this committee has no concern for the safety of this nation's citizens?
One	Possible, probable, definite. The committee was started to create something great

in this world and for the longest time the United States of America has been a force for good in the world. The people in this country are just like the people in every other country. What makes us different is the way we control them.

Two — We are the last barrier against a tyrannical dictatorship in this great nation. If we are rendered pointless, I can see another Lenin, Castro, Mau, or Khan.

Four — Did it ever occur to you that we might be thinking and acting the same way those people you just mentioned?

Two — How so?

Four — The five of us are worried about keeping our jobs on this committee. It has been my experience that every person who ever focused their efforts on trying to keep their jobs, didn't. Everybody that focused on doing their jobs, did. Right now you four feel threatened and you are willing to do whatever it takes to make the threat go away.

One — You have lost your way and I am concerned about your value to this committee.

Two — Please understand that it is important that we agree to do what we must to save this government.

Three — I know you think that this current government could use some cleaning, but our strength stems from the cooperation of a few leading factions. If the elections go independent, it will be a free for all.

Four — Where in the constitution does it make mention of political parties, unions, or establishing revenue sharing agreements between any of them? Why is it necessary that elected officials come from the two major political parties?

Two — How did you get on this committee when you feel the need to ask such ridiculous questions?

Four — Just lucky I guess.

One — We have an agreement with the Republicans and we have an agreement with the Democrats. We do not have an agreement with the Independents. We have tried to organize the Independents so that we might get an agreement but so far have been unsuccessful. The committee decided before you got here to stop trying.

Two — Had the Independents been in power we would have never gone to the moon or never built an International Space Station.

Four — We do not know what might have happened if things have turned out differently. We do know how this is going to turn out if we do not reconsider all of the things we thought we knew.

One	Like what?
Four	The money trail shows a decrease in interest in supporting established dogma. The dogma of the Republican Party, the dogma of the Democratic Party, the dogma for Scientology. Further investigation shows an increased interest in understanding something that cannot be successfully countered with propaganda. The people are more interested in the truth than feeling good.
One	Our job is to reverse that trend.

Election Day minus 27 days

Weather Report Northfield, VT

Actual	Avg.	Record	
Mean Temperature	45 °F	48 °F	
Max Temperature	55 °F	59 °F	77 °F (1993)
Min Temperature	34 °F	38 °F	15 °F (1964)
Average Humidity	68		
Maximum Humidity	92		
Minimum Humidity	43		
Precipitation	0.00 in	0.12 in	3.02 (1956)
Sea Level Pressure	30.25 in		
Wind Speed	6 mph (WNW)		
Max Wind Speed	18 mph		
Max Gust Speed	24 mph		
Visibility	10 miles		
Events	None		

The Dr. Charles Lectures - Time Eternal (Not really)

POL4350 – Political Absolutes Lecture 10

Professor Bailey Charles

Dr Charles

Let the lying begin.

Not preaching to anyone about anything or talking about whether the King James Bible gets it better than NASA or any other scientific group, my journey so far still has me asking questions with the understanding that none of the answers I really need can come from something someone has written down already.

But, I have stumbled onto the idea that all of the stuff that I know of is connected to and by me in some way. I now ask the question about all the stuff before me because all that stuff is somehow connected to me.

If I am trying to understand how something got the way it did in a system I was working on, I tend to go back as far as I can. In some cases I can get back to the date of manufacture for each component in the system, including lot numbers and supporting vendors. Most of the time I don't really need to go back too far and couldn't if I wanted to because the record set is sparse and the immediate solution is to buy a new part and move on. But as a person who has some time on his hands and believes that the solution I implement in my life going forward be as informed as possible.

The basic sources are those that rely on very old books and those published works that test a specific hypothesis and report the results. Both of these sources have their value in that the old books are written from the heart and give us tremendous insight into the human condition and the scientific studies give us insight into the physical world. Since I am both a mirror-fogging-carbon unit and an emotional spirit with ideas, dreams, and memories, both sources are required to give me a more solid foundation as to what I am intended to do with my life.

All of the data I will be considering is believed to be true by the person who took the time to publish it. But that does not mean it is really true but it is the best I got right now and should be sufficient to give me a clearer picture. I will discard the inconsistencies and see what's left over.

We each arrive in this sphere of existence with a set of needs that will ensure our biological process will function for the expected duration of our stay. There are statistics as to how long we can expect to stay or the impact of deviating from the set of needs I just mentioned.

Throughout our lives we become conditioned to consider the counsel of others and in doing so we turn away from the source. It is in the silence hearing no voices that we hear the only voice we should be listening to. Unless, the voices we hear are singing "The National Anthem," "Oh Holy Night," "Danny Boy," "America the Beautiful," "Bridge Over Troubled Water," or "Hey Jude."

Thank you.

End of Lecture

Election Day minus 25 days

Weather Report Fujiwhara Beach, FL

Actual	Avg.	Record	
Mean Temperature	77 °F		
Max Temperature	83 °F	81 °F	89 °F (2002)
Min Temperature	71 °F	72 °F	68 °F (1996)
Dew Point	66 °F		
Average Humidity	71		
Maximum Humidity	86		
Minimum Humidity	57		
Precipitation	0.00 in		
Sea Level Pressure	30.03 in		
Wind Speed	12 mph (North)		
Max Wind Speed	15 mph		
Max Gust Speed	-		
Visibility	10 miles		
Events	None		

Pontification of the MickBill - True Justice

Cue Music.

Announcer	And now, this week's edition of Pontification of the MickBill.

The idea of justice has become so perverted that it is nothing more than celebration of over-inflated egos and the refusal to accept total responsibility for one's life. The idea someone deserves to be treated a certain way or deserves to be compensated for mistreatment is ridiculous to me.

I can't believe I actually said that, but in the extreme the idea has some merit. I was told that a key milestone in my spiritual journey was to never be offended again. Since I have no overt control of what's coming at me and attenuators only work for so long before they burn out, I wonder how I could live my life effortlessly in peace. What is becoming apparent to me now is that I can only be offended if I see or hear things I believe to be offensive. This gives me two axes to which I can focus.

One axes pertains to the proximity to which I am located with respect to a source of offensive content. The second axis deals with my threshold for attributing something as offensive.

I needed a ground-zero location in which nothing evenly remotely offensive could reach me. The only things that I could be offended by are the things that I was imagining. This ground-zero location is any place that I am completely alone in my thoughts. It took a while to find this place and there are times I am further from it than I would like to be. The scariest times for me is when I think I am lost and can't get back to center. As soon as I stop crying, there it is.

The point is that for everything that is coming at us, our ground-zero location for inner peace is sometimes only a good cry away. When I was very young, I cried because the world was not the way I wanted it to be or that I was being mistreated. As an older man, I cry when I am filled with joy. Regardless of how old or young, I have a long record of looking for reasons to cry.

I learned in the service that crying is perfectly acceptable if you have a really good reason and the only good reason was that you are so overwhelmed with the passion you have for your chosen life and the love you feel for those who have answered the call to serve. When every waking moment is spent doing everything you can in service to others serving a common mission, you are living a life worth living and no injustice can fall upon you.

But I live in a close knit beach community with a very capable police force and don't get out much. How does my Zen bullshit stack up in south central Los Angeles or any location where there are many people living together? It stacks up perfectly.

I do what I can to stay close to my ground-zero location and only cry when it is a really good reason. It is an explainable rarity that I find myself even considering needing the services of an attorney. In my life, all of my interactions with attorneys have been to ensure full compliance with the law before I decide to do something.

But what about …? Look! I am not trying to convince you of anything. I am just telling you what I understand so far and have chosen to do with that understanding.

If you have been reading this book from the beginning, you should start to realize that the net direction a society went was determined by the collective thinking that began with one person writing it down or saying it out loud. So here goes:

Offenses and injustices are imaginary and sought out. The threshold is arbitrary and serves to distract people from living their lives with true purpose. If a person's actions have demonstrated an inability to live their life above the current threshold, that person should be summarily discarded without fanfare or malice. So unless you are willing to kill the person who offended you, quit crying. If you are willing to kill that person, I suggest you have a reason that a jury of your peers will think is a good one.

Everything else is one or more people crying about the world not treating them the way they think it should and every action they cite as justification could have been avoided. Where is the justice to be found when the person seeking justice is solely responsible for the offense?

Radical? Never work?

Whatever.

Everything happens exactly as it is supposed to under the circumstances. Change the circumstances, change the outcome.

Cue Music.

Announcer	This has been a Pontification of the MickBill.
Producer	And we're out.

Election Day minus 24 Days

Weather Report Fujiwhara Beach, FL

Actual	Avg.	Record	
Mean Temperature	77 °F		
Max Temperature	83 °F	81 °F	89 °F (2002)
Min Temperature	72 °F	72 °F	68 °F (1996)
Dew Point	63 °F		
Average Humidity	62		
Maximum Humidity	83		
Minimum Humidity	48		
Precipitation	0.00 in		
Sea Level Pressure	30.02 in		
Wind Speed	5 mph (NE)		
Max Wind Speed	9 mph		
Max Gust Speed	-		
Visibility	10 miles		
Events	None		

That Saturday Morning

TGTDTT	I got a call last night from FicChaSixteen that ended up with my sharing roasted chicken, avocado, hummus, and pita bread over a couple vodka tonics. The man announced he is running for Fujiwhara Beach City Council. I told him that if presented a petition to sign for him to get on the ballot, I will sign it. If I see his name on the ballot, I will vote for him. But that is all. I am out of politics and I will never write another check for a political candidate or movement ever again.
MickBill	That is harsh. How did he take it?
TGTDTT	It doesn't matter because this morning he will have no memory of the conversation or the decision to run for city council.
ShugaJoel	It seems a little late in the game to be considering entering the race. That said, the only other declared candidates are Good Ole Boys. Nobody wants to put up with the crap the "New Kids" did from the Good Ole Boys.
TGTDTT	FicChaSixteen is who I listen to when I think my frame of reference could be adjusted for a better view of what I am trying to see. I learned a long time ago that he talks. And that is all it is. Personally, I would love to see him on city council but not for the reasons he thinks I want him on city council.

MickBill	YouTube?
TGTDTT	YouTube.
MickBill	My picks have been published.
ShugaJoel	I have told everybody I know what I think they should do.
TGTDTT	And I hope it was to vote their faith that God doesn't want them to believe the fantasy that government can protect them and be the source of fulfilling their needs and desires.
ShugaJoel	Something like that.

Election Day minus 23 Days

Weather Report where the Committee meets

Actual	Avg.	Record	
Mean Temperature	66 °F	61 °F	
Max Temperature	69 °F	70 °F	89 °F (1962)
Min Temperature	62 °F	52 °F	31 °F (1906)
Dew Point	59 °F		
Average Humidity	81		
Maximum Humidity	93		
Minimum Humidity	68		
Precipitation	0.29 in	0.11 in	1.53 (1927)
Sea Level Pressure	30.08 in		
Wind Speed	11 mph (NE)		
Max Wind Speed	18 mph		
Max Gust Speed	24 mph		
Visibility	7 miles		
Events	Rain		

Homeland Security Summary to Committee

- Population deemed subversive to government remains within current guidelines if a Phase 1 lockdown were required.

- Seventy nine of one hundred voters align themselves with the current two party electoral system.

- The nationalization of industries abroad have exposed weaknesses in the control of sensitive information transmitted over the air or through a network.

- Threats of force to government are numerous. The extent of the threats is unknown.

- The single biggest threat to government is the upcoming nationwide election. It is possible, but not likely that independent candidates could replace party affiliated candidates in many critical offices.

Committee Meeting

Do we really know the professor is the source of our problem?

Five	I have never seen all the models converge in a singular long term prediction before. It is the reverse of a hurricane prediction. Sensitivity analyses performed on all adjustable coefficients rendered subtle shifts in the timeline, but never yielded a divergent solution.
Two	In English if you don't mind.
Five	The Dr. Charles Lectures are the source of the current threat. The quantified uncertainty is below the noise threshold.
Four	What about the next threat?
One	There will always be a next threat.

Election Day minus 20 days

Weather Report Northfield, VT			
Actual	Avg.	Record	
Mean Temperature	56 °F	46 °F	
Max Temperature	62 °F	56 °F	81 °F (1956)
Min Temperature	49 °F	35 °F	22 °F (2002)
Dew Point	52 °F		
Average Humidity	86		
Maximum Humidity	100		
Minimum Humidity	72		
Precipitation	0.00 in	0.12 in	1.77 (2010)
Sea Level Pressure	30.27 in		
Wind Speed	4 mph (South)		
Max Wind Speed	13 mph		
Max Gust Speed	17 mph		
Visibility	6 miles		
Events	Fog		

The Dr. Charles Lectures - Mindless Meanderings

POL4350 – Political Absolutes Lecture 11

Professor Bailey Charles

Dr. Charles

My lies have become so numerous, I can't even tell in my memory if I am telling a lie that I came up with or a lie that somebody told me. I guess if it makes a good story and you knew it was a lie to begin with, then who cares.

Depending on which actuarial table that is referenced, the remainder of my lifespan is expected to welcome at least one more new generation into this world and possibly as many as two.

The expectation that a transition from what we have now to what I dream can be completed in that time frame seems unrealistic under the best of circumstances. Taking into account my perceptions as to the general character of the current population and trending that towards subsequent generations reduces the likelihood even more.

"The America I will never know" is more of a statement as to what I expect to witness first hand than it is a statement of what is possible. The optimist in me believes it is possible, for no other reason than I had the thought and took the time to say it out loud for you to hear. With any luck, this talk will bolster the confidence of like-minded individuals and inspire a few that claim to be undecided.

Thank you.

End of Lecture

Fujiwhara Beach City Council Meeting

Pursuant to Public Notice, Mayor FicChaTwentySeven convened a regular meeting of the City Council in the Council Chamber. Those present were

```
Mayor FicChaTwentySeven,

Vice-Mayor FicChaTwentySix,

Councilwoman FicChaThirty,

Councilwoman FicChaTwenty,

Councilman FicChaTwoA,

City Attorney FicChaTwentyThree,

And City Manager FicChaTwoBee.
```

The mayor led a moment of silence and the Pledge of Allegiance.

The first order of business was the unanimous approval of breast cancer awareness month which is part of the propaganda movement to sway voter support for tax payer funding of twenty to fifty million mammograms every year. This is a sensitive issue for many people because few people over the age of thirty have not been affected by the disease. So maybe this is a good thing for government to do. Just don't forget that the government had no interest in getting involved until they realized it was the only way to tap into an industry that enjoyed tax exemptions and discounts. Private industry would have eventually found a way to capture the market without government intervention. The deal that was struck was a revenue sharing agreement that has kept the unit cost of a mammogram artificially high because the price is set by law. But since we are talking about our mothers, sisters, wives, let's let this issue pass as okay.

The next issue which passed unanimously was permission for the local soccer club to use the soccer fields owned and maintained by the city. From there, the council passed an ordinance entitled "Fertilizer Use on Urban Landscape" which restricts the use of certain fertilizers when there is a chance of storm water runoff into the lagoon. The city had to pass the law because the Environmental Protection Agency and the Florida Department of Environmental Protection said so. Now I can't say that I disagree. I can say that before it became a law, it was identified as a real problem that we caused and we could solve. Most of us showed that we weren't going to do what was best, so a few people convinced a few more people to get a couple of people to write some words that will justify recourse if we chose to continue to do the wrong thing. This is one of those times when government is really wanting to be smart and the people are incredibly ill-informed. But since the people have demonstrated consistently that they are ill-informed, all we can say is that this is one of those times when we all benefit if the lagoon's health is restored.

The fun started when the council considered the approval of the newly re-revised City Council Policies and Procedures. In this most recent revision, prohibitions on the type of speech or to whom it is addressed were put to the written word. There were some words that further restricted the conduct of individual council members. All the changes were made by FicChaTwenty. She was elected to govern, and govern she will.

The last item was the decision to pursue a ten thousand dollar grant with a five thousand dollar match that will be shared with a quasi-governmental organization for a study that will be conducted by the consulting firm of one of the board members on the quasi-governmental organization and managed by another one of FicChaTwoBee's sorority sisters. The motions were made and a four to one vote passed the expenditure of resources and the commitment of five thousand dollars so that there will be smiles all around the tailgate party this weekend for the last home game of the Florida State Seminoles. The study is to decide how to plan for coastal resilence. No, resilence is not misspelled. I had to look it up and if you are curious you might want to look it up as well.

FicChaTwentySeven The "Ayes" have it. The motion carries. That was the last item on the agenda. Meeting adjourned.

Election Day minus 18 days

Weather Report Fujiwhara Beach, FL

Actual	Avg.	Record	
Mean Temperature	78 °F		
Max Temperature	85 °F	80 °F	85 °F (2007)
Min Temperature	72 °F	70 °F	62 °F (2000)
Dew Point	71 °F		
Average Humidity	76		
Maximum Humidity	94		
Minimum Humidity	58		
Precipitation	0.00 in		
Sea Level Pressure	29.96 in		
Wind Speed	5 mph (NNE)		
Max Wind Speed	12 mph		
Max Gust Speed	-		
Visibility	10 miles		
Events			

Pontification of the MickBill - Purposeful Living

Cue Music.

Announcer	And now, this week's edition of Pontification of the MickBill.

If society is viewed in terms of a set of functional elements that work synergistically to accomplish something useful the way all the various parts of an automobile contribute to the end goal transporting people from one place to another, then it is possible to deconstruct all of the various elements in terms of their contribution to society. For instance, a police officer doing his or her duty each and every day contributes to an orderly and safe society. A teacher contributes to society through the imparting of knowledge and the inspiration of young minds. Ask the police officer, the teacher, or any number of other professionals the purpose they serve and they will more than likely have an answer that you can both understand and see merit.

What about those people who are clearly destructive elements that prevent a truly safe and orderly society? I am sure several examples have come to mind and I am spared the necessity to provide them. Do these individuals have a purpose that would justify their being allowed to walk the same streets as you and I? In the America of my dreams, the cost of housing, feeding, and guarding recidivists and first time offenders would be reduced to virtually zero.

We have given voice to the extremes of good and bad and now give some consideration to the middle ground. Those groups of people who are neither evil nor great have to be considered as whether or not they serve any purpose whatsoever. To imagine that I would be the one to decide whether anyone else in the middle ground has a purpose is a thought I cannot entertain, even as a fleeting fantasy. What I can offer is that if an individual's only concern is that they remain alive, they might want to visit the question as to why they should. If a person's only motivation is to receive that which they think they are due, then my hope is that they seriously question the merits of their continued existence.

To boil it all down, there is a group of clearly valuable people who need to be here and I am glad they are. There is also a group of people who clearly do not need to be here and, in the America I dream of, these people would be permanently and irrevocably removed to never be spoken of again. This last group, which makes up a too-large portion of our society, is unable to be judged by anyone other than himself or herself. In the America of my dreams, those people would take a hard and honest look at the lives they lead and either realize the value they bring, change their lives in a way that makes them clearly valuable, or do us all a favor and voluntarily depart the scene in such a manner that no one is inconvenienced.

There have been times in my life that I knew exactly why I was alive and there have been times when I was less certain. There have been a couple of times when my lack of certainty went to such extremes as to allow for the possibility of that voluntary departure I mentioned in the previous paragraph. But as I considered that possibility, I was confronted with an inner knowing that I was not "done yet." Even though I had no idea as to what it was I was supposed to do, I knew that it would come to me and I had to keep forging on. Maybe I would never do anything great with my life but I would do as many things as I could that I thought were good in some way.

In the America I dream of, everybody would wake up each day and commit themselves to making progress. Sometimes giving a stranger reason to smile when they would otherwise frown is progress. Allowing a car to change lanes so that they can make their exit or turn is progress. Telling a friend that you are grateful to have them in your life is progress. There are so many examples of small acts of kindness that make all the difference in a person's day. In the America I dream of, no one would feel inclined to have to tell someone do any of those things because people would already be doing them. In the America I dream of, there are no government programs that would take the place of a person giving of themselves in the service of others.

Cue Music.

Announcer	This has been a Pontification of the MickBill.
Producer	And we're out.

Election Day minus 17 Days

Weather Report Fujiwhara Beach, FL			
Actual	Avg.	Record	
Mean Temperature	79 °F		
Max Temperature	84 °F	79 °F	89 °F (2007)
Min Temperature	74 °F	69 °F	64 °F (2000)
Dew Point	72 °F		
Average Humidity	76		
Maximum Humidity	90		
Minimum Humidity	66		
Precipitation	0.00 in		
Sea Level Pressure	29.98 in		
Wind Speed	6 mph (SSE)		
Max Wind Speed	12 mph		
Max Gust Speed	-		
Visibility	10 miles		
Events	None		

That Saturday Morning

It is not that I am tired of writing dialogue, it is just that sometimes the essence is drowned out by the spoken word. This is one of those times. The upcoming elections were the dominant subject on everybody's mind but there was really nothing new to say on the matter except gossip, innuendo, and propaganda. Everybody sitting at the table that morning were happy to just enjoy the morning.

TGTDTT	What finally happened with McDermant?
MickBill	There are deals to be made.
OBandSD	"Endless Summer" is being shown tonight at DaVine's.
TGTDTT	The M*A*S*H of surfing movies that make the Haoles think their cool.
MickBill	What is with you?
TGTDTT	I am bored. This getting involved in the election to some extent is interesting in the same way football season is interesting. I am supposed to do something a little more meaningful than trying stop things by supporting a candidate.
OBandSD	How about supporting an idea and spending the rest of your life nurturing that idea. It is what I do.
MickBill	Says the man who lives in a camper trailer with no power or water parked in the side yard of a buddy.

TGTDTT	Don't be so fast to judge or discount. There is timeless wisdom in OBandSD's words. Words that I have known for many years but had forgotten. Thank you for the reminder. The check is mine this week.

Election Day minus 16 Days

Weather Report where the Committee meets

Actual	Avg.	Record	
Mean Temperature	60 °F	58 °F	
Max Temperature	67 °F	67 °F	88 °F (1938)
Min Temperature	53 °F	49 °F	30 °F (1880)
Dew Point	51 °F		
Average Humidity	68		
Maximum Humidity	84		
Minimum Humidity	52		
Precipitation	T in	0.11 in	2.73 (1906)
Sea Level Pressure	29.90 in		
Wind Speed	7 mph (SSW)		
Max Wind Speed	20 mph		
Max Gust Speed	26 mph		
Visibility	10 miles		
Events	Rain		

Homeland Security Summary to Committee

- Population deemed subversive to government remains within current guidelines if a Phase 1 lockdown were required.
- Seventy eight out of one hundred voters align themselves with the current two party electoral system.
- The nationalization of industries abroad have exposed weaknesses in the control of sensitive information transmitted over the air or through a network.
- Threats of force to government are numerous. The extent of the threats is unknown.
- The single biggest threat to government is the upcoming nationwide election. It is possible, but not likely that independent candidates could replace party affiliated candidates in many critical offices.

Committee Meeting

How far is the operation in place?

Five	The elements are in place, or will be in place, when the time arrives.
Two	Just out of curiosity, how does this all work?
Five	There are an infinite number of potential solutions for the intersection of two moving bodies when none of the variables or coefficients have been defined. As the range of variability is reduced and a subsequent optimization of the coefficients is performed in a loop fashion, the solution is obtained.
Two	In English please.
Five	I know exactly where all of the things we control are and I understand a time line for getting them to their exact locations so that the solution is correct. We have identified a set of solutions that represent the optimum scenario for our interests. There are efforts in place to guide the target toward one of those locations. As the target position is changed, intent can be established and we deploy our resources accordingly. This goes on until the only point of contact with the target body is made.
Three	Can't we just shoot the guy?

One	Dr. Charles must go to God in a way that conveys it was God's will. That is our only way of survival. Any hint that we were involved could spark a fire we won't be able to extinguish.

Election Day minus 13 days

Weather Report Northfield, VT

Actual	Avg.	Record	
Mean Temperature	44 °F	44 °F	
Max Temperature	54 °F	54 °F	80 °F (1979)
Min Temperature	34 °F	33 °F	15 °F (1959)
Dew Point	37 °F		
Average Humidity	70		
Maximum Humidity	86		
Minimum Humidity	53		
Precipitation	0.02 in	0.11 in	0.55 (1969)
Sea Level Pressure	29.81 in		
Wind Speed	7 mph (SSW)		
Max Wind Speed	18 mph		
Max Gust Speed	26 mph		
Visibility	10 miles		
Events	Rain		

The Dr. Charles Lectures - Prayer

POL4350 – Political Absolutes Lecture 12

Professor Bailey Charles

Dr. Charles

One of the biggest lies I like to tell is how I feel about prayer. So here goes.

From what I can tell from the prayers I have heard or read, I am supposed to begin with something that pays tribute to God's infinite nature. But what is the point in doing that? Even the word "infinite" comes short of really appreciating God. I don't even know if the word "God" is a good enough word. But since I grew up with the word "God" and there doesn't seem to be a real need to try and find a better word, let us be clear that when I use the word "God" I am talking about the source from which all reality comes forth.

The possible difference in my "God" and your "God" is that my "God" doesn't care. My "God" is God. I do not see a paradigm that involves my being worthy of God's Love. I do see a paradigm with respect to the extent I am manifesting God's Intent through the manner in which I spend this time on earth.

Assuming the paradigm I see as one that deserves consideration, the question that begins to appear has to do with the intention of my prayer. Anything I might ask for assumes that the source of its manifestation is outside of me. As I have unconditional faith that I am endowed with everything I need to manifest God's Intention as only I can, there is nothing I can justifiably ask for. There is a great deal I can justifiably do. But nothing I can ask for.

When I am unclear as to what I should be doing, I recognize it is because I am not listening to the voice of God as it is channeled through me. It is in this mode that my unconditional faith includes the provision that all of the questions I may have are accompanied by a unique and correct answer that will be revealed to me when I am willing to see it.

Most of the time, my prayers are like everybody else's prayers and not the kind of prayer I just described. And, for the most part, praying the typical way works pretty well. The barrier is the idea that God is out there and not in here (pointing to me). Remember that the goal is to allow God's intention, and all that comes with it be channeled through me as only I can.

So on the subject of prayer, I submit that living in the moment to make others feel less burdened, is the best a person can do in this life and God has given us everything we need to keep getting better at making others feel less burdened.

The only thing left to ask for is something that God has nothing to do with and that is money. Money that we need to pay the politicians who have promised to make certain people feel less financially burdened; Money that we want in order to live a certain way in a certain place; and money we think we would put to good use if we had it.

However, the Lord's Prayer is a really sound mantra to get your head pointed in the right direction. The Prayer of Saint Francis is also a really power syllabic offering that inspires positive emotion and harmony. Psalm 23, to include the version a dear friend of mine learned while in the service, is also a pretty good patch of words to utter in times of contemplation or doubt. There are any number of good prayers that will help calm the mind and prepare a person for whatever is next. If you take the time to pay attention to the words, the prayers all say that "surrendering to God's intention" is a choice that good people make. That surrendering includes giving full credit where credit is due.

Thank you.

End of Lecture

Election Day minus 11 days

Weather Report Fujiwhara Beach, FL

Actual	Avg.	Record	
Mean Temperature	72 °F		
Max Temperature	76 °F	79 °F	88 °F (2007)
Min Temperature	69 °F	69 °F	53 °F (2006)
Dew Point	57 °F		
Average Humidity	59		
Maximum Humidity	77		
Minimum Humidity	51		
Precipitation	0.00 in		
Sea Level Pressure	30.10 in		
Wind Speed	14 mph (NNW)		
Max Wind Speed	17 mph		
Max Gust Speed	17 mph		
Visibility	10 miles		
Events	None		

Pontification of the MickBill - Utopia

Cue Music.

Announcer — And now, this week's edition of Pontification of the MickBill.

"...We hold these truths to be self-evident, that all men are created equal, that they are endowed by their Creator with certain unalienable Rights, that among these are Life, Liberty and the pursuit of Happiness ... " is the beginning of the second paragraph to the Declaration of Independence that is commonly considered the document that marks the beginning of the United States of America. Common thinking is that it was signed on July 4, 1776 but that thinking is false. Regardless of when it was actually signed by the representatives of the Continental Congress, it is where I begin my journey of defining a nation that is worthy of God's love and protection.

The America in my dreams allows for each individual to pursue their individual destiny in a way that enhances the lives of all those in their vicinity. The citizens of the America in my dreams are compelled by an unrelenting inner force to live each and every day in the service of the greater good by bringing their individual talents to the forefront for exploitation without fear or selfishness. The industries of the America in my dreams are committed to making the very most of the resources this rich land provides while at the same time protecting and nurturing those resources so the environment is healthy and brings forth life in abundance. The local, state and federal governments of the America in my dreams ensure that international commerce is fair, that our infrastructure is sound, and that our citizens are free to manifest their God given destiny. The military of the America in my dreams eradicates all foreign elements that bring harm to the citizens of my America.

People will live each day to its fullest with no sense of entitlement but a complete commitment to being the best they can be in service to others. Businesses will be committed to products and processes that make the world a better place. Governments will be focused on roads, bridges, treaties, and the removal of individuals who endanger productive citizens. A military will be trained, equipped, and led in such a manner that a call to arms by my government will compel immediate surrender by those who act to harm us. These are the composite elements of the America in my dreams.

The America in my dreams is a kind nation to those who have earned kindness yet can bring forth a wrath like no other when conditions warrant. When its citizens seek to harm other citizens, they are summarily removed from the citizenry and never spoken of again. In the America of my dreams, narrow and small-minded people are free to crawl into a deep hole and remain silent when their thoughts are destructive but are dealt with quickly and permanently when their actions attempt to demean other human beings.

Freedom of speech is celebrated to the extent that we are speaking the truth when we attempt to represent information as fact. Freedom of religion is celebrated, but there are no protections or special considerations for religious practices. Individual liberties are protected as sacrosanct to the extent that those liberties make no infringement on the personal liberties of others. Government's power is limited to those activities that benefit all citizens and cannot be accomplished by the private sector commercial interests or individual citizens.

The aforementioned seems rather idealistic, but without idealism we have no hope of ever experiencing an America where all of us embrace the responsibility of doing our very best and realizing our individual potential in the service of others.

Cue Music.

Announcer	This has been a Pontification of the MickBill.
Producer	And we're out.

Election Day minus 10 Days

Weather Report Fujiwhara Beach, FL

Actual	Avg.	Record	
Mean Temperature	72 °F		
Max Temperature	78 °F	79 °F	86 °F (2003)
Min Temperature	67 °F	69 °F	51 °F (2005)
Dew Point	58 °F		
Average Humidity	63		
Maximum Humidity	78		
Minimum Humidity	47		
Precipitation	0.00 in		
Sea Level Pressure	30.20 in		
Wind Speed	12 mph (NNW)		
Max Wind Speed	16 mph		
Max Gust Speed	20 mph		
Visibility	10 miles		
Events	None		

That Saturday Morning

TGTDTT	It occurred to me that the probability of a tyrannical dictatorship would seem inversely correlated with the percentage of the population that understands mathematics and physics.
MickBill	What about history, social studies, civics?
ShugaJoel	What about English?
OBandSD	History is what we decide it is. All of the other stuff you mentioned has to do with governing the masses. I am not sure math is the ticket. I get what you have been saying but I don't get math.
TGTDTT	But you get physics.
OBandSD	Not like you get physics.
TGTDTT	My job has always been to make sure that I was ready for the future that was coming. Whenever I was asked to look at something that was wrong, I turned my attention towards understanding the chain events and eventually identify the root cause. My thesis is that our burdens would be somewhat relieved by a growing number of young people who understand that decisions based on some reasonable effort to quantify the variables have a better chance of getting them where they want to go. The reason things are the way they

	are now is that people read or hear words and then believe them. The words they are being told are lies and would see it if they would do the math.
MickBill	I don't need to do the math to know what is right or to do the right thing.
TGTDTT	But you will need math to understand how much stuff you will need to get the right thing done.
MickBill	That is a good point. So what are you suggesting or saying.
TGTDTT	What say you to the idea that I will devote the rest of my life to the spreading of the gospels according to LaPlace, Euclid, Descartes, Newton, and many other wise seekers of truth?
OBandSD	College level?
TGTDTT	High School.
MickBill	Good luck with that.

Election Day minus 9 Days

Weather Report where the Committee meets

Actual	Avg.	Record	
Mean Temperature	46 °F	56 °F	
Max Temperature	57 °F	65 °F	82 °F (1978)
Min Temperature	35 °F	47 °F	28 °F (1879)
Dew Point	29 °F		
Average Humidity	58		
Maximum Humidity	82		
Minimum Humidity	33		
Precipitation	0.00 in	0.10 in	2.65 (2007)
Sea Level Pressure	30.15 in		
Wind Speed	10 mph (SSW)		
Max Wind Speed	24 mph		
Max Gust Speed	32 mph		
Visibility	10 miles		
Events	None		

Homeland Security Summary to Committee

- Population deemed subversive to government remains within current guidelines if a Phase 1 lockdown were required.

- Seventy seven out of one hundred voters align themselves with the current two party electoral system.

- The nationalization of industries abroad have exposed weaknesses in the control of sensitive information transmitted over the air or through a network.

- Threats of force to government are numerous. The extent of the threats is unknown.

- The single biggest threat to government is the upcoming nationwide election. It is possible, but not likely that independent candidates could replace party affiliated candidates in many critical offices.

Committee Meeting

One We expect the balance of power will remain in eighty four percent of the governed regions. The places where it shifted don't have an impact on the Electoral College. In short, we are still one hundred percent in control.

Four I do hope you take the time to record the date and time you just said that.

Two You have a different view.

Four If you question the extent to which you are in control, you are not in control. The mere thinking that you are in control nullifies whatever control you thought you had. Believing you are in total control of externalities is the ultimate hubris.

One I tire of your insolence and defeatist attitude.

Four You believe One is a superior number to Four.

One It is not a belief. Tradition has always put One at the head of the table.

Four If an event is the result of choice, it is not a truth. A truth will stand up to infinite scrutiny. All you have to argue is "That is how it has always been." You have lost the way.

One I am the way!

Three	Let's not get too carried away here. We are all under a great deal of stress. This will be over in a little more than a week.
Two	The worst thing any person can do is to think they have won before the battle is over. I caution all of you to revisit your priorities and refocus on the task at hand.
Five	But who is going to plan for tomorrow?

Election Day minus 6 days

Weather Report Northfield, VT

Actual	Avg.	Record	
Mean Temperature	29 °F	41 °F	
Max Temperature	41 °F	51 °F	70 °F (1989)
Min Temperature	16 °F	32 °F	16 °F (2013)
Dew Point	19 °F		
Average Humidity	70		
Maximum Humidity	96		
Minimum Humidity	44		
Precipitation	0.00 in	0.10 in	1.32 (2003)
Sea Level Pressure	30.46 in		
Wind Speed	1 mph (West)		
Max Wind Speed	8 mph		
Max Gust Speed	12 mph		
Visibility	9 miles		
Events	Fog		

The Dr. Charles Lectures - Prayer of Saint Francis

POL4350 – Political Absolutes Lecture 13

Professor Bailey Charles

Dr. Charles

I have a feeling that my lying days are almost over. But as I have been wrong about so many things, I could be wrong about this. There is also the well-established fact that I am lying to you, have been lying to you, and will continue to lie to you as long as you are within a comfortable speaking range. I wear this microphone thingy so that you people in the back row can hear me lying. I can see by the little lights on your mobile phones that some of you are recording the lies that I have told and the ones I will be telling during this lecture. I am in awe at the lengths people will go to make sure a lie is well recorded. Now let's get to work.

Francis of Assisi was a Catholic monk who cast aside the trappings of his family's wealth and lived the remainder of his life in commune with nature as the ultimate celebration of God's Love. The prayer that is named after him goes something like:

Lord, make me an instrument of your peace,

Where there is hatred, let me sow love;

Where there is injury, pardon;

Where there is doubt, faith;

Where there is despair, hope;

Where there is darkness, light;

Where there is sadness, joy.

O Divine Master,

grant that I may not so much seek to be consoled, as to console;

to be understood, as to understand;

to be loved, as to love.

For it is in giving that we receive.

It is in pardoning that we are pardoned,

and it is in dying that we are born to Eternal Life.

Amen.

Or put another way,

Lord, all I am really asking for is that I am not the biggest asshole in any room with more than one person in it. I will do all I can to stay on the path that you are laying out for me but will stumble from time to time. It would be of great help if my stumbles never make the evening news, the subject of a "60 Minutes" episode, or an incident report to the Office of Academic Protocol. All of the rest of the time, just help me understand how to be a better dude.

The idea that giving all of ourselves to the pursuit of being a good person as the path for Eternal Life is just another piece of text that reinforces the idea that when I do the thing I am supposed to do the way I am supposed to at the time I am supposed to, I get to graduate.

The first twelve or so years of my life, I was happy and clueless for the most part. During years 13 through 18, I was just trying to survive. Years 19 through 53, I was making something of myself. Now it is time to really do something with my life or have I done enough and can just coast the rest of the way? Either way, my efforts must be a truly sincere service to others or I am just wasting everybody's time.

Thank you.

End of Lecture

Election Day minus 4 days

Weather Report Fujiwhara Beach, FL

Actual	Avg.	Record	
Mean Temperature	80 °F		
Max Temperature	84 °F	77 °F	84 °F (2003)
Min Temperature	77 °F	67 °F	54 °F (2012)
Dew Point	68 °F		
Average Humidity	68		
Maximum Humidity	81		
Minimum Humidity	57		
Precipitation	0.00 in		
Sea Level Pressure	30.10 in		
Wind Speed	13 mph (SE)		
Max Wind Speed	15 mph		
Max Gust Speed	20 mph		
Visibility	10 miles		
Events	None		

Pontification of the MickBill-Role of Government

Cue Music.

Announcer — And now, this week's edition of Pontification of the MickBill.

The role of government is to be the central point for collection of taxes and distribution of those revenues in a manner that benefits all citizens for those things that individual citizens cannot provide for themselves. National Defense is something that benefits all citizens. Border patrol and Law Enforcement benefit all citizens. The Department of Transportation does things that benefit all citizens such as the construction and maintenance of highways and bridges, but beyond that, the DOT does a lot of things that are best handled by the private sector. The Department of Education as a data collection entity to gage the performance of our various educational institutions benefits all citizens but the role they play in the mandating of curriculum and selective distribution of taxpayer revenues does not. A similar set of statements can be made about virtually every other government agency at the Federal level. By and large, the federal government takes care of all of those things that benefit all citizens but engages in activities that the private sector and individual citizens would handle better.

The federal government should purchase the goods and services from the private sector that it needs to operate but it should not bail out companies that have been mismanaged or become obsolete. The federal government should have a tax policy that applies to all citizens, close all loopholes, and not act as a bank for startup companies intended to serve the private sector.

A similar set of statements may be made about state, county, and municipal governments, except on a progressively smaller scale. Government is necessary to maintain an orderly society but when it controls society or attempt to offer services that benefit society, it is over-reaching. If done right, the free market and entrepreneurialism will take care of most of the problems government attempts to solve.

Here are some examples of what government attempts to solve, but doesn't:

- Poverty
- Unemployment
- Drug abuse
- Illiteracy
- Prejudice
- Homelessness
- Teenage pregnancy
- Gay marriage and adoption laws

The reason that government has failed to really solve any of those problems, is that it can't. Government makes a behavior illegal or legal and incorrectly assumes that such laws solve a particular problem. The reason is that it doesn't solve the problem is that it attempts to legislate how to be innovative in either thought or deed by setting forth requirements that inhibit innovation and action.

You may disagree, but the Civil Rights Act of 1964 didn't end prejudice. President Johnson's War on Poverty hasn't ended poverty. The mortgage laws intended to force banks to finance homes people couldn't afford did nothing to stop homelessness. The "No Child Left Behind" Act has not made the nation more literate. In most cases, actions taken by government only made things worse or had no impact at all.

The role of government is to pass laws that can be framed in terms of theft from one person by another person, to make sure that our toilets have some place to flush to, and we have roads to drive on. Going much beyond those simple examples is activism, which is best, left to private citizens. The following are examples of things government should do:

- Build Roads and Bridges
- Make sure the Intra-Coastal is navigable
- Prevent bad things and bad people from entering the country
- Destroy governments that have attempted to destroy ours
- Arrest, provide trials, and process criminals
- Install sewers, public drinking water, electricity, and telecommunications services
- Settle disputes between citizens

If the role of government is framed using the words should or better, then it is over reaching. If the role of government is framed using the words fixed or complete, then it is probably a proper role.

As far as laws are concerned, if the universal penalty for violating a law is death, my suspicion is that lawmakers would be reluctant to engage in futile exercise of social engineering. As far as justice is concerned, a civil court system will deal with those matters that involve people who have been treated unfairly.

Cue Music.

Announcer	This has been a Pontification of the MickBill.
Producer	And we're out.

Election Day minus 3 days

Weather Report Fujiwhara Beach, FL			
Actual	Avg.	Record	
Mean Temperature	81 °F		
Max Temperature	89 °F	77 °F	89 °F (2013)
Min Temperature	73 °F	67 °F	59 °F (2012)
Dew Point	70 °F		
Average Humidity	73		
Maximum Humidity	90		
Minimum Humidity	47		
Precipitation	0.00 in		
Sea Level Pressure	29.97 in		
Wind Speed	9 mph (SSW)		
Max Wind Speed	17 mph		
Max Gust Speed	-		
Visibility	10 miles		
Events	None		

That Saturday Morning

ShugaJoel	Can you believe this weather? When does fall get here?
OBandSD	This time of year is my favorite. The evening breezes air out the land barge.
MickBill	Have the neighbors complained about your snoring?
OBandSD	I don't complaint about theirs. They don't complain about mine.
FicChaTen	FYI guys. The cat is out of the bag and everybody at this table might want to avoid FicChaTwelve's wife ... I know I am.
TGTDTT	You guys have her all wrong. Deep down inside she knows that good men get called to duty. She's been married to him since way back in his Air Force days. I am not going to avoid her. When I speak to her, I am going look her right in the eyes.
FicChaTen	What is it with you trying to protect her or make excuses for her? Is there something you want to share?
TGTDTT	You guys forget that this is her hometown. She has heard every single bit of gossip about people in this town by the people in this town. She has seen the gossip turnout to be true and she has seen it turn out to be lies. She knows the kinds of things people are capable of saying in this berg ... and

she has been the target of it in the past, driving her to tears. Plus the whole thing about her husband getting fired and all because he was asking the wrong questions of the wrong people.

MickBill	How's your buddy doing on his quest to sit in the chair at the front of the room with the adults?
TGTDTT	I don't know. If I see his name on the ballot, he gets my vote. Other than that, I have been busy with other things I believe are of greater value.
FicChaTen	Care to share?
TGTDTT	I just got my substitute teaching certificate in the mail and now I can get started on nailing down a permanent certificate to teach math and physics in one of the local high schools.
MickBill	Good for you?
TGTDTT	We'll see.

Election Day minus 2 Days

Weather Report where the Committee meets

Actual	Avg.	Record	
Mean Temperature	62 °F	54 °F	
Max Temperature	72 °F	63 °F	85 °F (1971)
Min Temperature	52 °F	45 °F	28 °F (1923)
Dew Point	45 °F		
Average Humidity	62		
Maximum Humidity	84		
Minimum Humidity	40		
Precipitation	T in	0.12 in	0.99 (1940)
Sea Level Pressure	29.74 in		
Wind Speed	7 mph (NW)		
Max Wind Speed	22 mph		
Max Gust Speed	30 mph		
Visibility	10 miles		
Events	Rain		

Homeland Security Summary to Committee

- Population deemed subversive to government remains within current guidelines if a Phase 1 lockdown were required.

- Seventy six out of one hundred voters align themselves with the current two party electoral system.

- The nationalization of industries abroad have exposed weaknesses in the control of sensitive information transmitted over the air or through a network.

- Threats of force to government are numerous. The extent of the threats is unknown.

- The single biggest threat to government is the upcoming nationwide election. It is possible, but not likely that independent candidates could replace party affiliated candidates in many critical offices.

Committee Meeting

One	I have to ask.
Five	I have to leave you in suspense.
Three	Will both of you stop your childishness?
Four	Have you all heard of a Banyan Tree?
Two	Your point?
Four	You should not plant one next to your home.
Two	I think your real point is how robust they are with their root structure and regenerative capability.
Four	Maybe, but I would have told it better.
Five	(Hanging up his mobile phone) All is in place.

Election Day

Weather Report where the Committee meets

Actual	Avg.	Record	
Mean Temperature	43 °F	54 °F	
Max Temperature	49 °F	62 °F	84 °F (1974)
Min Temperature	36 °F	45 °F	26 °F (1879)
Dew Point	22 °F		
Average Humidity	45		
Maximum Humidity	56		
Minimum Humidity	34		
Precipitation	0.00 in	0.11 in	2.30 (1970)
Sea Level Pressure	30.60 in		
Wind Speed	8 mph (NE)		
Max Wind Speed	17 mph		
Max Gust Speed	22 mph		
Visibility	10 miles		
Events	None		

One	The polls close at seven this evening, we should know the results by nine, unless there are races too close to call.
Three	Everybody in this room knows that. Why did you just make that announcement?
One	There is something that everybody in this room does not know.
Two	What is that?
One	The Homeland Security predictions.
Five	How are they different than what the Associated Press is reporting?

One	The goal of the associated press is an interesting and accurate story. The goal of Homeland Security is to identify potential threats to government. Homeland Security drills down through every government office all the way to the voters.
Four	What do our friends at Homeland Security say?
One	The report says that elected offices will primarily be held by representatives of the two major parties.
Two	Is that all?
One	It is the way the predictions were worded. Since Homeland Security started paying attention to how election results might be deemed a threat to the government, they have always given a statistical breakdown with respect to the likelihood that one or more of the candidates was a potential terrorist or subversive. This report is a message that the power the two major political parties now hold is at risk in the foreseeable future.
Two	By the mere act of putting word to thought, you have sealed our fate.
Three	This is not the first time we have faced such things and it will not be the last. In the long run, we will get to back to controlling things either way. I am just wondering if we can use these developments instead of trying to stop them. We all know how this ends if we try to implement the kinds

	of controls needed. How much death do you want to cause?
Four	Do any of you allow for the possibility that our democracy began with unofficial alliances based on ideas and that this is nothing more than a move back in that direction. You all have become entrenched in your thinking as a controller that you look for things to control. You fight this and we will all be on the wrong side of history.
One	Mind your words my young friend. There are some in this room that might get the wrong idea about what you're saying. Speaking only for myself, I sense a hint of surrender on your part.

The committee was in disarray. None of them were wrong within their frame of reference. But there was no common frame of reference. Until there was an agreement on the frame of reference, there could be no consensus as to the best course of actions.

The data mining activities of Homeland Security are mathematically perfect in the sense that the math is right. But correlation is not causality. There are a number of similarities in the mathematical properties of the trended rise in Independent voters and the rise in viewership of The Dr. Charles Lectures. But to say that one was caused by the other is a leap of faith.

But how much data and how much data crunching is enough so that a decision can be made? The only way to test causality is to introduce a known change into the source and then measure the output. No one in the room had any ideas how to test for causality. Few in the room would even give the idea any thought whatsoever. Besides, the instructions to the people who work for very important people were already being carried out.

Election Night Part 1

Weather Report Northfield, VT			
Actual	Avg.	Record	
Mean Temperature	25 °F	40 °F	
Max Temperature	36 °F	49 °F	71 °F (1982)
Min Temperature	14 °F	30 °F	14 °F (2013)
Dew Point	15 °F		
Average Humidity	65		
Maximum Humidity	92		
Minimum Humidity	38		
Precipitation	0.00 in	0.11 in	1.60 (1983)
Sea Level Pressure	30.69 in		
Wind Speed	1 mph (NW)		
Max Wind Speed	9 mph		
Max Gust Speed	12 mph		
Visibility	10 miles		
Events	None		

Traveling east on highway 302 in eastern Vermont, Dr. Charles was reliving his youth driving his sun faded blue '96 Camaro Z28 that he bought almost two decades ago. Even though there was more wrong with it than the paint job, the car reminded him of a happier time when he was working on the space shuttle program. He had been toying with the idea of retiring the car and could see himself in a Cadillac Escalade. Getting something new, or at least newer than the car he was driving, made sense because the defroster in the new car would probably work.

Bailey Charles hand wiped the inside of the windshield using a couple of paper napkins from the bag of drive thru food in the seat next to him. As he was dealing with the immediate concern associated with an inadequately performing windshield defroster, he knew that he should do something before the serious cold weather started.

Flying above Bailey's car at about one thousand feet was a reconnaissance drone that was transmitting signal intelligence and targeting data back to central control. The data was processed using an algorithm developed by a professor under the auspices of solving a control systems problem for an anti-dampening system to be used by the International Space Station.

Stripping away the nuances of how such a system would actually work, the principal equation defines the application of force in three dimensional space by two moving bodies. If the routes of the two bodies are known and the positional vector of the target body is known, a solution that involves having the control body impact the target body with maximum impact is obtainable.

This was not the first time the system was ever used, but it was the first time it was used within the United States of America. The thinking of the planners was that once the target had committed to a particular route that would take him to Maine, there were several controlled opportunities that carried a good chance of success.

The professor who developed the algorithm that solved the equation for what was about to happen was promoted to Dean of Research.

The control body was a modified tanker carrying ten thousand gallons of ethyl alcohol. At the moment of impact, the container of alcohol burst followed by ignition of a series of incendiary devices mounted on the control body one second after impact. In the cab of the control body was an adequately documented cadaver, to make the overall event look like a truck driver who fell asleep at the wheel.

The chosen target intercept point was at a two-way stop at the bottom of a valley. The east-west path had a clear shot, the north-south traffic was expected to stop. The visibility of the intersection coming from the west gave a driver less than one point four seconds of reaction time for a perfectly timed intercept at maximum velocity of the control body.

Dr. Bailey Bernard Charles ceased to exist in the physical sense less than 90 seconds after final approval was given. Six days after he gave his final lecture. One month since he had last seen his brother. A lifetime without knowing the love of a woman. The college will make an announcement, the local papers will render the explanations that should satisfy the masses, unless the calculus has changed, the Committee should feel relieved.

Target intercept occurred at 1342EDT. The 911 call reporting the incident occurred at 1349EDT. Emergency services first responders were on site at 1411EDT. By 1414EDT, the accelerants had been consumed and the fuel source was limited to the unburned flammable materials such as the oil, tires, plastics, and paint. The first approach to the passenger area of either vehicle occurred at 1420EDT. Each vehicle was found to be occupied by a single person in the respective driver's seat. The condition of the corpses were essentially burned beyond recognition and pronounced dead at the scene.

The vehicle identification numbers led the authorities to trace down the path to the college president to understand that Dr. Bailey Charles was the driver of the smaller vehicle. The driver of the larger vehicle led to a series of phone numbers until a voice told the authorities that the driver of the vehicle was a contracted driver and was given another number to dial. After a few more numbers were dialed, the local police department received an email that contained a copy of the driver's license of the person said to be the contracted employee and a phone number to dial in case of emergency. The emergency number led to a voice that that gave instructions what to do with the remains and where to send the death certificate.

At 1730EDT the college president sat down at his computer and composed an email to the post master of the He Man Woman Haters Club in Fujiwhara Beach. The email announced Dr. Charles's accident and death. That email was forwarded and reproduced. The forwarded emails and reproductions were forwarded and reproduced. At 1802EDT, TGTDTT received one of the forwarded emails, then another, and another. At 1805 EDT, there was a knock at the door.

Stranger	You are wrong when you think that no one knows who you are or cares what you do.
TGTDTT	You judge me and you warn me.
Stranger	It is the person I work for. Now that you know, you must decide.
TGTDTT	I hate making decisions.

Election Day plus 1 Day

Fujiwhara Beach City Council Meeting

Pursuant to Public Notice, Mayor FicChaTwentySeven convened a regular meeting of the City Council in the Council Chamber. Those present were

Mayor FicChaTwentySeven,

Vice-Mayor FicChaTwentySix,

Councilwoman FicChaThirty,

Councilwoman FicChaTwenty,

Councilman FicChaTwoA,

City Attorney FicChaTwentyThree,

And City Manager FicChaTwoBee.

The mayor led a moment of silence and the Pledge of Allegiance.

There was a crowd tonight in celebration and gloat. The Police Chief formally recognized city volunteers of distinction. The City Manager recognized the Police Chief for being selected to the State Executive Board of Director's as the 3rd Vice President of the FBI National Academy Associates. The first item that required a vote was the certification of the election results.

FicChaThirty — I make a motion that we approve the results of the election.

FicChaThirty's motion to call the election certified caused rumbles in the room. Mostly supportive rumbles. Sitting in the front row with a smile on his face was FicChaSixteen. He was flanked by his loving special person and a half dozen people who stepped up to show support. But he knew this council. He knew that if FicChaTwenty did not like the way something turned out using her rules, she would rewrite the rules and make them retroactive (democracy wasn't her strong suit). In his case, he knew that FicChaTwenty had some other tools in her tool box just to make it painful. Since the City Clerk only released the unofficial results, she could demand that the council wait until the official results are published by the Supervisor of Elections. FicChaSixteen had been a thorn in FicChaTwenty's side for quite a few years. She was not going to let him sit up there with her without putting up a fight. FicChaTwenty quickly spoke up.

FicChaTwenty	I move that we wait until the official results have been published.
FicChaTwentySix	I second the motion. Not the one to wait, but the first motion. The one to certify the results ourselves and get back to work.

This is one of those times when I could describe for you what was happening in the room or I could leave it to your imagination. I am going to slide somewhere in the middle, between just writing what they said to each other, and describing in detail the rise in cortisone levels in FicChaTwenty's bloodstream and the impact on her response to the recent developments.

Suffice it to say, there was a collective gasp in the room. It was the first time in a long time that any of the four other council members showed any support for FicChaThirty. What elevated the event to "You had to have been there" status was that the support for FicChaThirty's motion was in direct defiance of FicChaTwenty's stated intentions. Everybody in the room knew who controlled the council and now FicChaTwentySix was standing on his own. The poor mayor just did not know what to do. Once the mayor appreciated what was happening …

FicChaTwentySeven	A motion has been made and seconded. I call for a vote. I'll vote last.
FicChaTwentySix	"Aye"
FicChaTwenty	"Nay"
FicChaTwoA	"Aye"
FicChaThirty	"Aye"
FicChaTwentySeven	I vote "Aye," the "Ayes" have it. The motion carries. That was the last item on the agenda. Meeting adjourned.

FicChaTwoA was happy to vote "Aye" because he was a FicChaTwenty appointee almost two years ago and was happy to have his first and third Wednesdays free again. FicChaTwentySeven always voted the prevailing winds. This was the first time since taking office two years ago that he did not know the vote results before the meeting even started.

FicChaSixteen, after years of speaking into the microphone on the podium, now gets a seat at the table. TGTDTT is considering filming a documentary of his term in office. It will be called "Bring it Forward" as an homage to something he said at least three times in every conversation that lasted more than one minute. This would include the three minutes he was given every single time he spoke at the podium. His campaign slogan was "Bringing it forward." "Bringing it forward" is all anyone can ever remember him ever saying. So I guess it helped with name recognition when it came time to read the ballot.

Election Day plus 3

Weather Report Fujiwhara Beach, FL			
Actual	Avg.	Record	
Mean Temperature	74 °F		
Max Temperature	80 °F	76 °F	84 °F (2003)
Min Temperature	69 °F	65 °F	52 °F (2010)
Dew Point	69 °F		
Average Humidity	87		
Maximum Humidity	100		
Minimum Humidity	69		
Precipitation	0.00 in		
Sea Level Pressure	30.02 in		
Wind Speed	7 mph (NNW)		
Max Wind Speed	12 mph		
Max Gust Speed	-		
Visibility	8 miles		
Events	None		

Pontification of the MickBill – Farewell to Dr. Charles

Cue Music.

Announcer — And now, this week's edition of Pontification of the MickBill.

Of the many tragedies on Election Day, one that has only been reported via emails, blogs, chatrooms, and now this radio show is that Dr. Bailey Bernard Charles has given his last lecture.

I call on all my listeners to watch The Dr. Charles Lectures on YouTube.

My regular listeners know that I have never endorsed or mentioned a particular person unless I saw a way it would work out well for me. I offer no explanation because the mere mention of Dr. Charles Lectures causes a flag to go up in some data tracking software run and created by the National Security Agency. Maybe it is good that Homeland Security is using a good net to catch the bad buys before they do bad things. But a good friend told me that believing something has a quality, does not change its essence. Besides, he told me, nobody really cares what I think anyway.

So what do you say to we all stick it to the man by checking out those lectures and then getting your friends and family to check them out as well? Let's raise so many flags at the National Security Agency that the President of the United States, every person elected to congress, every elected state official, every elected county official, and elected city official all understand that we know what you are doing, we know why you are doing it, and we are willing to live with some of it. But you are overplaying your hand and you are making promises that are way above your pay grade to keep. It won't happen overnight, but with each election comes a voter block that will not support the corporate candidate that continues to grow government.

The more we elect candidates who are committed to stripping down government to its bare essentials, the better we will all be as human beings.

The ripples of the election that we just had three days ago are set in motion. It is time to turn our attention on how we will impact the election just two years away.

Cue Music.

Announcer	This has been a Pontification of the MickBill.
Producer	And we're out.

Election Day plus 4 Days

Weather Report Fujiwhara Beach, FL

Actual	Avg.	Record	
Mean Temperature	74 °F		
Max Temperature	78 °F	76 °F	87 °F (1996)
Min Temperature	69 °F	65 °F	50 °F (1997)
Dew Point	66 °F		
Average Humidity	76		
Maximum Humidity	88		
Minimum Humidity	66		
Precipitation	0.00 in		
Sea Level Pressure	30.07 in		
Wind Speed	14 mph (North)		
Max Wind Speed	25 mph		
Max Gust Speed	31 mph		
Visibility	10 miles		
Events	None		

That Saturday Morning

TGTDTT	Post game analysis shows something pretty interesting.
MickBill	It shows that the Republican Party of Florida has lost touch with its base and its values.
TGTDTT	Independents were the spoilers for the incumbent in ninety percent of the elections held nationwide when the two party split was less than twenty points.
MickBill	Everybody knows they are spoilers which is why most people don't vote for them.
TGTDTT	You are missing the point. All of the election reporters and the reports are based on the two party system. On Election Day, more people defected in the voting booth than before. But that is not the best news.
MickBill	Which is.
TGTDTT	Two years ago, the spoiler threshold was ten points. Two years before that it was five points. Let us assume for a moment that something good is happening. The first question is "What is it?" The second question is "How do we help it?"
OBandSD	We can't. At least not in the various ways it has been tried before. If we do that, someone is going to identify at least some of us as some kind of leader. Once that

happens, the movement is over and evolution is quashed for a while.

What we need to do is to understand how we seem to be aligned with the change and improve that understanding. We can go paddling around looking for opportunities to drop in or we can be patient. Because we have listened and sought a path towards seeing and hearing clearer, we are in the best place we could possibly be at this moment. If the voice of self begins to speak, we may not hear the voice that has brought us to this place.

ShugaJoel — What on earth are you talking about?

TGTDTT — What my spiritual and ethereal friend is saying is that the establishment of a celebrity is the only way any movement can be hindered or destroyed. The last thing any of us should be doing is telling people they listen to what we have to say. Besides, the first thing people will start to paint you with is the image of David Koresh or James Jones. No, No, No. Don't follow me, don't listen to what I have to say, and for goodness sake; don't think I have the answers to whatever problems you think you have. OBandSD suggests you all do the same.

MickBill — I still don't know how this all ends.

OBandSD — It doesn't end. It evolves. When I think about it, it seems like the rate of evolution of human consciousness would be pretty constant if it weren't for our inclination to hold on to disproven ideas. Then things get pent up and we noticeably evolve. Then we get comfortable. But the impetus for evolution is constant. Your comfort will not change the schedule and you will need to run to catch up if you stop to take a break. You would understand that if you surfed.

ShugaJoel — I surfed all the time as a kid.

OBandSD — Yeah and you understood then what I am saying now.

Election Day plus 5 Days

Weather Report where the Committee meets

Actual	Avg.	Record	
Mean Temperature	45 °F	52 °F	
Max Temperature	56 °F	61 °F	79 °F (1994)
Min Temperature	34 °F	43 °F	26 °F (1976)
Dew Point	28 °F		
Average Humidity	54		
Maximum Humidity	75		
Minimum Humidity	32		
Precipitation	0.00 in	0.10 in	1.40 (1889)
Sea Level Pressure	30.24 in		
Wind Speed	9 mph (SSW)		
Max Wind Speed	20 mph		
Max Gust Speed	24 mph		
Visibility	10 miles		
Events	None		

Homeland Security Summary to Committee

- Population deemed subversive to government remains within current guidelines if a Phase 1 lockdown were required.

- Seventy out of one hundred voters align themselves with the current two party electoral system.

- The nationalization of industries abroad have exposed weaknesses in the control of sensitive information transmitted over the air or through a network.

- Threats of force to government are numerous. The extent of the threats is unknown.

- The single biggest threat to government is the upcoming nationwide election. It is possible, but not likely that independent candidates could replace party affiliated candidates in many critical offices.

Committee Meeting

How far do you want to keep going?

Five	I have new analysis results.
Two	We thought you might.
Five	First I want to report that the retirement of Dr. Charles had the expected result. By applying the theorem of known results to our models, we were able to run a new set of scenario analyses and see if there is any semblance of convergence. There is not at this moment.
One	There is more.
Five	Because Dr. Charles made the choices he did, we were able to better model that lattice. In doing that, we identified certain patterns that started to align in terms of what might happen. When we use those patterns in our scenario analysis, all of the models converge again.
Four	How many layers in your decision lattice?
Five	Each layer has multiple sub layers the same way a set of stairs are effectively the same as a set of floors but they lead to the next layer or level.
Three	Does your decision lattice support regression.

Five	The decision lattice does not allow for time to stop or go backwards if that is your question. There is no going back. What we seek to do is to establish a set of conditions that have similarities to periods when the government was under less threat.
Four	Check your history. Every generation produces a government that causes the people to make noise. The only time they are quiet is when someone else is shooting at them. Where is a good Hitler wannabe when we could use one? The best we have right now are radical Islamic fundamentalists and trying to get the world to go after the conservative wing of Islam is an almost impossible task.
Two	What did you find out?
Five	There is a guy on AM talk radio in Florida that might get some traction if we don't intervene.
One	What is his name?
Five	MickBill.

Election Day minus 719 Days

Weather Report Fujiwhara Beach, FL

Actual	Avg.	Record	
Mean Temperature	70 °F		
Max Temperature	74 °F	75 °F	82 °F (1997)
Min Temperature	66 °F	63 °F	59 °F (2002)
Dew Point	54 °F		
Average Humidity	54		
Maximum Humidity	61		
Minimum Humidity	47		
Precipitation	0.00 in		
Sea Level Pressure	30.25 in		
Wind Speed	17 mph (ENE)		
Max Wind Speed	21 mph		
Max Gust Speed	29 mph		
Visibility	10 miles		
Events	None		

Pontification of the MickBill

Cue Music.

Announcer	And now, this week's edition of Pontification of the MickBill.

I know something most of you don't know. I can't tell you what it is, even if I wanted to. Because I know what I know, I now know that I do not know. My lack of knowing extends to the inability to know that I do not know. With that being said, I just want you to enjoy to my show.

Which, by the way is brought to you by the show's newest sponsor which I am not allowed to mention on the air or in private if I want to keep my job or stay alive.

Let me just say that I enjoyed that brief period when I forgot how completely full of crap I am. I am serious. I am full of crap. My doctor says to start a fiber regimen and eat more salads, but I like a good burger and those fiber powders give me gas. The orange stuff doesn't taste too bad. Speaking of orange stuff, our beloved Homeland Security Agency has upgraded the terrorist threat level to orange. So be on alert when you are out and about. Don't forget to report any suspicious activity to your local authorities. Just remember, we are all in this together.

Cue Music.

Announcer	This has been a Pontification of the MickBill.
Producer	And we're out.

Election Day minus 718 Days

Weather Report Fujiwhara Beach, FL

Actual	Avg.	Record	
Mean Temperature	72 °F		
Max Temperature	76 °F	75 °F	84 °F (2008)
Min Temperature	69 °F	63 °F	55 °F (2000)
Dew Point	64 °F		
Average Humidity	72		
Maximum Humidity	83		
Minimum Humidity	56		
Precipitation	0.02 in		
Sea Level Pressure	30.15		
Wind Speed	10 mph (East)		
Max Wind Speed	14 mph		
Max Gust Speed	21 mph		
Visibility	0 miles		
Events	None		

That Saturday Morning

Every story has to come to an end. Good stories make you want to hear more. Bad stories make you grateful that it is over. The merits of the story teller are to be defined by what the reader feels and does next based on how well the story was told. A good story teller would end the story in a way that makes you wonder if there is possibly more stories down the road. Here is my attempt at doing just that.

MickBill	I see we have a guest this morning.
TGTDTT	You can see him?
MickBill	Of course I can see him. Hello. I am MickBill.
FicChaZero	Hello. I am ...

Just as FicChaZero began to speak, Holly started talking to MickBill. This gave TGTDTT the time to process why MickBill can see FicChaZero. Holly can't see him, or at least if she can, she won't let on. She took MickBill's breakfast order and went on her away. She never acknowledged FicChaZero's presence in any way.

MickBill	So, what brings you to our humble gathering? Oh, I did not catch your name.
TGTDTT	That is my fault. MickBill, meet FicChaZero. FicChaZero, meet MickBill.

MickBill turned to FicChaZero in search of an answer to the remaining question on the table. FicChaZero understood.

FicChaZero	TGTDTT has started to invite me on more of his errands and appointments. You are

the first person to ever even notice I was in the room.

TGTDTT — There are less than two years until the next time government will be rebooted and loaded with new software.

MickBill — There is a honeymoon period. The holidays. The self-congratulatory statements to the people. Then back to the politics.

TGTDTT — Just as disappointment and/or frustration can take the place of faith in you, faith in you can take the place of disappointment and or frustration. In this matter, there is a dichotomy whose resolution is singularly dependent on an individual's world view.

FicChaZero — What cracks me up is that I was here before any of you and I will be here long after you have let loose the mortal coil and humans don't get that. It is as if there is some kind of game that they might win or that they can be a more dominant force than I can be. Maybe in the short term, but not for any sustained period of time. An island nation might have a better chance of remaining under an oppressive god/government than some place that borders other places. But in the end, all life comes from, through and to me and humans seem to think they can ignore that.

MickBill — I am sorry. Did you just say what I think you said?

FicChaZero — Everything I have ever said has been what you think I said.

TGTDTT — This is what I expected. Everything is just fine until you think that FicChaZero thinks that he is who you think he is. What you have to understand is that FicChaZero can only be who you think he is and that is your choice. But whatever traits or properties you conjure up for this FicCha, it only reinforces its fictionality and becomes a source of suspicious activity inquiries with the people at Homeland Security.

MickBill — Who is FicChaZero to you?

TGTDTT — I am not having this conversation because it is the wrong conversation. Instead of worrying about who I think FicChaZero is so you can compare it with who you think FicChaZero is, just listen to what FicChaZero tells you and get on with your life. If you make FicChaZero the story, you will cause death and destruction.

MickBill — That is a little dramatic, don't you think?

TGTDTT — First of all, I am not saying I am right about anything and I am not asking anybody to think what I think or believe what I believe, or anything else. But if I am right, the reason that I am here is to be a conduit for the types of messages that caused crucifixions, inquisitions, reformations, revolutions and many other unpleasant chapters in our past. If I am right and I never believed it then my soul is clean. If I believe it, right or wrong, my soul is tarnished by ego. In such a case, I would then be a distraction from evolution. Regardless of whether I am right or wrong, ask yourself what happened the last time the noise levels got this high at the federal, state, county, and local levels. Then ask yourself what happened to get everyone to shut up.

MickBill — I have known you for a few years and I have always thought you were an independent thinker, but you have crossed the David Koresh threshold for saying outrageous things and I can't go where you are trying to take me or my show.

TGTDTT — You told me yourself that the goal of the show, next to being marketable, is to be entertaining. Do you not find this entertaining?

MickBill — I don't think my audience will understand or find this amusing.

TGTDTT — So we don't go on your show. But I know you are going to think about what has been said.

The End.

Final Thoughts

There will be more to come. More that I have to come to understand in my heart and can hear the voice that attempts to articulate it. I sometimes like to watch how the sentences and words create patterns on the screen as I type. Then I begin to hear the music that speaks to the lyrics arising from the words that I have typed and I am inspired to bring it all together into one grand finale.

But that is what you would expect of me. Had I not known that, you would be experiencing the grand finale right now. Such as it is.

TGTDTT is beginning to understand that his calling may include the role of high school math and physics teacher. It is his belief that if people understand how the world really works, they would not get conned into what people are trying to sell them, especially in government where assets are seized and people can be imprisoned. Teaching only mathematics and physics, with no commentary as to how the world should be, TGTDTT believes he can do what he loves and benefit others. Should he find himself meeting the same fate as Dr. Charles, so be it.

MickBill has been put on notice and he has made his decision for now. There may come a time to take a stand but it is not today. He can still do and say about eighty seven percent of what he would want to do and say, so what is the big deal. He rates his job as a B plus. At least he is working.

OBandSD had to explain to the Fujiwhara Beach policeman that he did not realize the neighbors had trimmed the shrubbery that usually concealed the fact that he showered outside. The extent of the trimming was such that it would be spring before OBandSD took another shower. There was an undiscussed competition among the four other members of the Saturday morning group for the upwind seats. Swirling winds brought no relief from the stench of man's arrogance in thinking that trimming his hedges back was the right thing to do. To this day, I do not believe this neighbor has any idea as to the far reaching consequences of his actions.

FicChaTen wakes up each morning, looks in the mirror, and reminds himself that he is doing the right thing or he tries to remember where he is. He prefers the mornings spent trying to remember where he is because it means he got a good night's rest and his life up this point really has been a hell of a dream.

There is young man who seeks to be a Florida Representative for either District 52 or 53 (he hasn't decided, but he has promised to actually live in the district he ends up representing). His showing for his efforts this time around were respectful for a first timer but it was not the Cinderella story some had hoped for. It is possible that TGTDTT will play a role in his life, but who is to say. Only God can say but I can't hear him right now because everybody else is talking to me.

FicChaThirty returned to her life as Citizen FicChaThirty.

FicChaTwenty, FicChaTwentySix, and FicChaTwentySeven have two more years left on their terms. FicChaTwoA was the second of two candidates for the open seats. There was no election so he is in for another four years.

FicChaTwelve saw his name on the big screen one more time with less than one percent of the vote. Every single person that loved him and believed in him wrote his name on the ballot for Senate District 16. I won't tell you how many it was but suffice it to say that he was moved to inconsolable tears of humility. His wife breathed a tentative sigh of relief.

FicChaSixteen is bringing it forward.

The End.

Cast of Characters

FicChaZero	Whomever the reader decides the character is.
FicChaTen	See Volume 17.
FicChaTwelve	Mild mannered, quiet, well intentioned guy who somehow gets talked into things. SeeVolume 17.
FicChaThirteen	See Volume 17.
FicChaSixteen	See Volume 17.
FicChaTwenty	See Volume 17.
FicChaTwentySix	See Volume 17.
FicChaTwentySeven	See Volume 17.
FicChaThirty	See Volume 17.
FicChaTwoA	See Volume 17.
FicChaTwoBee	See Volume 17.
MickBill	AM Radio morning Talkshow host. See Volume 17.
TGTDTT	The Guy that Does The Thing. See Volume 17.
OBandSD	Old Beach and Surfer Dude. See Volume 17.

Fujiwhara Beach	See Volume 17
Mosquito County	See Volume 17
GSofFL	Great State of Florida. See Volume 17.
MCFLMosFB	Municipal Corporation Florida Mosquito County Fujiwhara Beach. See Volume 17.

Exhibits

The item(s) that follow are a strikingly similar representation of the real thing if you actually went looking for it.

School Resource Office Program Goals

1. To identify and prevent, through counseling and referral, delinquent behavior, including substance abuse.

2. To foster a better understanding of the law enforcement function.

3. To develop positive concepts of law enforcement.

4. To develop a better appreciation of citizens' rights, obligations, and responsibilities.

5. To provide information about crime prevention.

6. To provide assistance and support for crime prevention.

7. To promote positive relations between students and law enforcement officers.

8. To enhance knowledge of the fundamental concepts and structure of the law.

9. To annually evaluate the effectiveness of the program based on input from students, parents, the school staff, and the community, and submit a written report to the principal.

10. To provide materials and consultative assistance to teachers and parents on various law education topics.

More by W. C. Andrew Groome

"*The Guy That Does The Thing – Observations, Deliberations, and Confessions Volume 17*"; ©2014; iUniverse; ISBN:978-1-4917-2006-6; www.TheGuythatDoesTheThing.com

"*Ripple*" ©2012, Tate Publishing & Enterprising, LLC; ISBN: 978-1-62024-157-8; www.RippleTheBook.com

"*Collection and Analysis of Wideband Measurements from Two 850 MHz IS-95 CDMA Systems Using the Berkeley Varitronics Shifting Correlator PN Scanning Receiver*" © 1998, Florida Institute of Technology